Rave Reviews

—*Esquire*

"A graphic satire of bedroom mores."
—*The New Yorker*

"Deft satiric wit."
—*The New York Times Book Review*

"Masterfully told… Phillips keeps it compelling
to the end."
—*The Seattle Times*

"Irresistible."
—*J.D. Landis, author of* Longing

"Inventive, vividly written… highly entertaining."
— *Kirkus Reviews*

The one with the big watch put a hand on my chest, and I stopped and looked down at it.

"That's a mistake," I said. "Undo it."

"We need to talk a minute, Mr. Rose," he said.

"You don't look like much of a conversationalist. Take that hand away."

"Listen, friend," he said. "We need to talk about how you talk to people."

Maybe it's because I was such a lousy boxer, but I don't see the point of going move and countermove with people who ought to know the moves as well as you do. What I'd rather do is upset the board. I gave out a sort of groan and began to sit down, as if I were tired or having an attack, and without thinking the pug tried to pull me back up again by the tie. All two hundred forty-odd pounds of me, one-handed. I almost felt sorry for him. But I came up again fast, grabbing the back of his neck as I went, and broke his nose with my forehead. The pug fell back clutching his face and screaming way back in his throat, and his buddy moved in, but glancing over at his friend instead of tending to business, and I kicked out sideways and broke the buddy's knee. That would have settled me for a while, but he looked like he wanted to get up again somehow, and I kicked him in the belly, which made him more introspective. By this time the first guy had gotten out his gun and lit off a couple, clutching his face and firing half-blind...

Fade to
BLONDE

by **Max Phillips**

A HARD CASE CRIME NOVEL

A HARD CASE CRIME BOOK
(HCC-002)
September 2004

Published by

Dorchester Publishing Co., Inc.
200 Madison Avenue
New York, NY 10016

in collaboration with Winterfall LLC

This book is a work of fiction. Names, characters, places, and incidents either are the products of the author's imagination or are used fictitiously, and any resemblance to actual events or persons, living or dead, is entirely coincidental.

ISBN 0-8439-5350-0

The name "Hard Case Crime" and the Hard Case Crime logo are trademarks of Winterfall LLC. Hard Case Crime Books are selected and edited by Charles Ardai.

Printed in the United States of America

Visit us on the web at www.HardCaseCrime.com

FADE TO BLONDE

I

Blue Convertible

Well, maybe she wasn't all that blonde, but it'd be a crime to call hair like that light brown. It was more sort of lion-colored. Lioness. It was heavy, shiny hair, and it fell straight down to her shoulders from a central part. She hadn't done much to it. She didn't have to. She got out of the big Studebaker convertible and walked across the red dirt where someday there was supposed to be a front lawn. I was up on the roof, laying tile for one of those little hacienda-looking breadboxes. The whole street was full of them, all half-built. She wore a pale blue dress with cream piping, a dark blue belt, and a silly little schoolgirlish collar. She had nice straight shoulders. There was nothing wrong between them and her open-toed shoes, so I guess the trouble must have been somewhere behind those blue-gray eyes. There'd be trouble, of course. She looked up and called, "Is your name Corson?"

I said it was.

"Are you busy?"

I didn't think she could be an actual movie star. She didn't walk right, and she was too thin for the work, with two notable exceptions. She looked up at me, shading her eyes. "I'd like to talk to you."

"You are," I said.

"I might have some work for you."

"What kind?"

She just stood there, looking up at me. "Well, you're big enough," she said at last.

I kept waiting.

"I hear you did some boxing," she said.

I kept waiting.

"It looks like you got hit."

"Not really," I said. "I went nine and two. I broke the nose falling out of a tree in third grade. The rest of the face has just always been that way."

I was annoyed with myself. No one needed to hear any of that.

"I still think you've been hit a few times," she said, smiling faintly.

It was actually a pretty nice smile.

I walked over toward the carport to where the roof swooped down low, and sat myself down on the edge. She came and stood below me, between my feet. She was a tall one, all right.

"I've been hit a few times," I said.

"Nine and two's not bad. Why'd you stop?"

I shrugged. "They started to match me with guys who knew how to box. And it wasn't what I came here to do."

"What did you come here to do?"

"Why don't you keep telling it?"

"You came here to write. For pictures. But you didn't have any luck. You did a few treatments for Republic and Severin gave you a few scripts to read. He liked you, there were a few of them who did, but he didn't know quite what to do with you. He gave you extra work and a few bit parts. You even had a line in one. You were the palooka the promising young boxer knocked out in the first reel. What was your line, by the way? If you don't mind my asking?"

After a minute, I said, " 'So you're the Kid. They tell me you're pretty good.' "

She smiled again, still faintly. She was still looking up from between my feet, shading her eyes. When one arm got tired, she'd use the other hand. "I'm getting a crick in my neck."

"I'm comfortable."

She patted my boot. "I just don't want you to kick me in the face. At least not until we've been properly introduced."

I slowly pushed my boot out toward her chin, and she walked backward to keep ahead of it, her hands clasped behind her hips, smiling faintly up at me the whole while. When she was back far enough, I jumped down. "Thanks," she said. "Can we talk somewhere private?"

"This is private," I said.

She looked up the street. "Yes. I guess it is. You seem to be the only one working this morning."

"The contractor's going bust. Our pay's been late."

"But you're still here."

"I like to keep busy. Who's been singing my praises?"

"A man named Reece who does security at Republic."

"How do you come to know Mattie?"

"He's not difficult for a girl to know," she said. "When the acting didn't work out, you tried a little bodyguarding."

"If you want to call it that. I put on a suit and stood around behind some guys. Every once in a while I'd lay my hand on someone's shoulder and give him the look."

"Show me," she said.

The hell, if that's what she wanted. I reached out and let my hand fall on her shoulder. I gave her the look.

She clasped her hands together and laughed delightedly. "I take it all back. You *are* an actor. Unless you really want to beat my head in with a pipe wrench and dump my body in a ravine?"

"Not until we've been properly introduced," I said. "Anyway, that's not what the look says. The look says, Are you sure you want me to kill you with a pipe wrench and dump you in a ravine? Because I'd really rather not be bothered."

"Yes. You're right. That's what the look says."

"What's your name?"

"Rebecca LaFontaine."

"What's your real name?"

"It's not very pretty."

"Yeah, well. Still."

"Out here, I go by Rebecca LaFontaine."

"Where are you from? Middle West someplace?"

"That's close enough."

"Why'd you come here?"

"Why does anybody come here?" She shrugged. "It didn't work out. I can't act. I got some offers. Of a certain kind."

"But not for movies."

"I got offers for movies of a certain kind."

"But none you wanted to do."

"No," she said steadily. "I did a couple. I don't want to do that again."

I looked up the street. It was still just a dirt track. You could hear the whisper of the cars from the freeway across the valley. It was one of those bone-dry days when sound travels. There were big rolls of cyclone fencing lying around, I don't know what for. No one had bothered to put them up. I looked back at her and said, "That's terrible. You know where they're showing any of them?"

"You wouldn't recognize me," she said. "I parted my hair differently back then. Look, let's not keep standing around like this. Let's go sit in the car."

She turned and walked off. After a moment, I followed. She got in on the driver's side, and I rode shotgun, if we were riding. The seats were white vinyl and already hotting up in the sun. She took hold of the steering wheel, closed her eyes, and let her breath out through her nostrils. Then she gave the wheel a little pat and dropped her hands in her lap. "So. You're a screenwriter, an actor, a bodyguard. And a roofer, too."

"I do odd jobs."

She said, "I want a man killed."

"Not that odd."

"I didn't mean that. Not killed, really. Just hurt."

"I'd think you could do that work yourself."

"Or scared."

"Like I said."

"I'm serious. There's a man who's, who's got to leave me alone. I don't know what to do about him. I need someone to help me."

"What's he doing?"

"I can't tell you that unless I know you'll help me."

"Does it have to do with those movies?"

"It has to do with a lot of things. I can't tell you unless I know you're with me."

"What do you do for a living?"

"Like you. Odd jobs."

"Such as "

"Sales clerk, lifeguard—I swim pretty well. Hatcheck girl. Perfume girl. One of those girls who stands around department stores smiling, with a bottle of perfume, and asks if you want a little puff. I tried modeling, but clothes don't fit me."

"Where'd you meet this man?"

"I was a hat check girl."

"That pay pretty well?"

"No."

"Nice car."

"He didn't buy it for me, if that's what you mean. My folks left me a little money, and I came out here and got a place and bought a car, because I thought it would help, you know, to look right. The car's what's left. I can't even afford to have it washed."

"Why don't you sell it?"

"I did. To him. He holds the note on it now."

"But he lets you go on driving it."

"He says one night when I'm out miles from any-where, he'll pull up behind me at a light and make me get out and give him the keys. And then I'll have to walk home. In my high heels and little dress. So that by the time I get home, my feet will be bleeding and my stock-ings will be torn and my legs will be black with dust, and my face, and I'll stink with sweat like a farm animal, like a cow, which, you see, is all I am, and I won't be pretty any-more. Except he knows I'll hike up my skirt to get a ride from somebody, some, um, farm hands—yeah, that's about right—and be taken into some field and, and raped by the whole bunch of them, one after another, raped to death, which I'll love, because that's the kind of skinny bony filthy whore I am."

"Nice," I said.

"He really is crazy, but he's got a business and I don't suppose he wants that interfered with, so there must be some way to reach him. Don't you know how to do things like that? Mattie seems to think so. He's got to leave me alone. He's got to stop threatening me. Just when I'm beginning to get somewhere and get myself normal for once."

"You could've picked someone else to sell your car to."

She let her head flop back against the seat. "Well. You know. He used to be very sweet." She reached out a knuckle and rapped me softly on the chest. "I've been hit a few times, too," she said.

Her eyes were large, pale, and set wide beneath a broad, low forehead. Her chin was pointed, but her fine-lipped mouth was wide. There wasn't really room for it on her face, any more than there was room for that chest on her skinny frame. Her arms and legs were too long. Sitting there behind the wheel, she looked like she'd folded them up the wrong way, the way you'll fold a road map the wrong way. I could see why she'd flopped in pictures. She was disturbing-looking. Ten thousand guys had made a play for her, but I don't guess any of them kidded himself it was a good idea at the time. I rubbed my face and said, "Let's see what we've got. There's a man, you'd rather not say who, and you want me to make him stop doing something, you'd rather not say what. Kill him, threaten him, you'd rather not say. And you'd rather not tell me your real name. And you're broke."

She opened her purse, took out what was in it, and gave it to me.

I counted it. "It's not much," she said.

"No," I said.

"But you'll take it?"

Way out on the freeway, I heard a car horn, very faintly. Somebody was losing his temper. Then the traffic was whispering along smoothly again. The sun felt good on my face. I could smell the hot vinyl seat and the girl sitting beside me with her fists in her lap, waiting. She didn't use perfume, just regular soap. I got out my wallet and tucked her money inside.

"Don't they always?" I said.

2

Chain

I watched her car out of sight, and then climbed back on the roof and finished the row. I didn't like to leave it all cranksided like that. To pass the time I thought what I sometimes do. I think, What if it was my house I was working on. I think about how I'd finish the roof, or the driveway or what have you, and how I'd get a truck then and move some nice furniture in, and hang up some curtains, and some pictures, and put some dishes in the cabinets and some food in the fridge, and how it'd be done then, my house, and how me and some nice woman would move in and live our lives. I didn't think about moving in with Rebecca while I was finishing the last row. I wasn't that dumb, not yet. So the little woman didn't have a face or name, but I'll admit she did wind up on the tall side. When I was done I stacked up the loose tiles for the next guy, if there was one, and gave each of my tools a wipe with an oily rag as I put it away. I like a good set of tools. I closed the toolbox and climbed back down, leaving the ladder where it was. There was supposed to be a truck coming by each evening for things like that. I put my tools in the trunk of my car and went to see the boss.

Ortiz & Son had a little office in Inglewood. It was basically just a gravel parking lot with a wire fence around it, big enough for a couple of cement mixers and a few cars and, in the corner of the lot, a two-room shack. One of the rooms was so the laborers would have somewhere to wait for the truck. The other was for Nestor Ortiz. From what I hear, old Ortiz had always been a stand-up guy, but he was gone now and if anyone had a good word to say about his son, they hadn't said it to me. Nestor Ortiz always wore a jaunty little porkpie hat with the brim turned down in front like a fedora. He was a dapper little guy, and he knew every man on every one of his sites by name, and their families' names, and he'd go around asking all the guys, How's your family. I don't have a family and it didn't sweeten me. When I opened the door, he spread his hands and said, "My friend! My friend, I know all about it."

"Hello, Nestor," I said.

"Raymond, my friend," he said. "I know all about it

and is terrible. I stand before you this moment in shame. In shame."

"It's been three weeks, Nestor."

"I know and is an awful thing. Awful. Everybody coming to see me, all good men like you, who work hard, and they need their pay, and what can I tell them? What? I'm not getting any money, I can't give any money, and I don't blame you one moment if you quit."

"I am quitting, Nestor."

"I don't blame you a moment."

"I still need my pay."

"And you gonna get it, every cent. But right now you got to be a little patient because it isn't so good. I can't pay I don't get the money from Olindas Estates. And where is Olindas now? Do they pay me? No."

"Nestor, you are Olindas. You're forty percent of Olindas."

"That's only forty percent," he said. "My friend, I assure you I am completely and totally and absolutely broke at this moment we're speaking."

"I've seen where you live, Nestor. Have you seen where I live?"

"I assure you it is impossible right now for me to pay everybody asking."

"I'm not asking you to pay everybody," I said, trying to get my breathing under control. "I'm asking you to pay me. Seventeen dollars a day times thirteen days. No, I quit early today. Call it twelve days. Two hundred and four dollars. This isn't the first time you've tried to short me, Nestor."

"I hear," he said patiently, "what you are saying. Do you hear what I am saying?"

"I did the work, Nestor. I want to be paid for it."

"Is that all you can say the same thing over again? I heard you already, your pay. I am trying to talk to you like a reasonable civilize human being. Can I do that, you think?"

"Nestor," I said.

The first time you use a jackhammer, your hands are so swollen at night that you can't close them. You can barely pick a fork up off the table. That's the way my whole head felt just then. That's how it takes me. It's as if the front of my brain was swelling, locking up, and all I could think was, *I want my pay. I want my pay.* I didn't blame Nestor for being sick of it. I was sick of it myself. I told myself to turn around and walk out. I wasn't listening. I leaned forward on my hands and took a breath. Nestor looked up at me, unimpressed. I said, "Nestor."

"Lissen, what do you want," he said. "Think about what you really want. You want me to call the cops, that what you want?"

"Yeah, you want the cops here, Nestor. You want them here real bad. Nestor, I'm telling you. Give me my goddamn money, all right?"

"And I am telling you, you are a goddamn big stupid *cabrón* of an ape. And you gonna wait for your pay a long time. And how 'bout *that*?"

All right. It was out of my hands now. Anyway, that's what I usually tell myself. The room was crammed full with rolls of tarpaper, coils of wire, cartons of bathroom tile. There was a two-foot length of heavy chain on the corner of Nestor's desk, an open padlock hooked into the last link. I unhooked the padlock, picked up the chain, and came around the desk. "Oh, now you're gonna be a big tough guy," he said. "Now you're gonna scare me. Big tough guy. Now you're gonna threaten." I scooped him out of his chair, mashed him one-handed against the wall, and wound the chain around his neck. His little hat fell to the floor. I slipped my fingers in between the chain and the side of his neck, gripped the chain, and twisted.

Nestor made a squeaking noise back in his throat, and then he made no noise at all except for the scuffling of his feet against the floor and the clacking of his teeth as he opened and closed his jaws. His bulging eyes didn't leave mine. They seemed to be searching for some sign that I was somehow kidding. I loosened the chain and said, "I want my pay, Nestor."

"You're crazy!" he croaked. His voice whistled in his throat. "Crazy!"

I tightened the chain again and he was quiet. He was staring into my eyes, and then he was staring past them. His little belly heaved convulsively and his fingers scratched at my chest. "I want my pay," I said.

I loosened the chain again.

"Crazy! Crazy!" he whispered.

"Two-hundred and four dollars," I said, towing him over to the desk by the chain. He scrabbled in a drawer and pulled out a checkbook. I took it and dropped it back in the drawer. "Checks can be stopped, Nestor."

He pulled his wallet from his breast pocket and threw it on the desk. He began to curse me in his whistling, broken voice. I tightened up a little and he stopped. "Count it for me," I said.

He had a hundred and thirteen dollars. I put it in my pocket. "All I got!" he shrieked. " 'S all I got!"

"Ninety one dollars more, Nestor. Halfway there. Where's the petty cash?"

He jerked open a desk drawer and threw a small lock-box on the desk. He pulled out a small key, unlocked it with trembling fingers, and thrust the box toward me. It skidded off the desk and spilled onto the floor.

"Pick it up," I told him.

He got down on his hands and knees and began scooping the money up and flinging it on the desk and chair, cursing me all the while in Spanish and English and maybe a few other languages. He was terrified of me, but he couldn't seem to stop cursing me. I knew how he felt. I let go of the chain and it slithered to the floor and landed with a clunk. I didn't see any singles on the desk, so I picked up four twenties and three fives and put them in my pocket. "Okay," I said. "Now we're quits."

He just sat there in a scatter of money, holding his throat and weeping. I'd expected a bald spot under the hat, but he had a nice head of hair. I set his hat back on his head. "See you, Nestor," I said.

He didn't look at me as I left. He was busy weeping. I'm not sure he knew I'd been there anymore. I'm not sure he remembered what had hurt him.

3

Reece

Back then I lived at the Harmon Court Motel, out on Harmon, near Paige. The place was right behind the Sun-Glo billboard, which was something of a local landmark. The Sun-Glo Girl was seventy-five feet long and lay around all day on an elbow and a hip. Her job was to lie there, smiling and brushing back her hair. From the front she was an awfully healthy-looking girl, but from my window all you could see was the plywood back of her, propped up by iron struts. It was still a pretty healthy profile. The Court was usually half-empty, but it didn't cost much to keep open, and I guess tearing the place down was more work than somebody was in the mood to do. My room was the last one past the pool. It was one of two deluxe rooms that had a kitchenette in the corner, and I got a percentage off my rent in exchange for handyman work. That was the theory, anyway.

When I got home from Nestor's office, I sorted the money out on the dresser: twenties, tens, fives, and ones. Two hundred and eight dollars. I added the money Rebecca had given me and counted again. It made a decent little pile. It wouldn't last, because I was behind seven weeks' rent and two payments on my car, but it still felt nice between my fingers. It's always good to get your pay. There was a mirror over the dresser, and I watched myself tuck the bills neatly in my wallet, and then I stood and looked at myself. I looked like the kind of guy who strangles contractors. I pulled off my clothes, turned the shower up as hot as I could bear, and stood under it awhile. I toweled off and had a drink from the bottle in the desk. I looked in the mirror again. Better. I put on some pants. Better all the time.

Aside from my clothes and groceries, the only things in that room I owned were the typewriter on the desk and a trunk where I kept my books. I didn't keep the books out on shelves because I didn't have any shelves, and because if girls saw them they wanted to talk about the pug who reads and wasn't that wonderful.

I only buy books by people I wish I wrote like. I had some Hawthorne, some Irwin Shaw, and some John Dos Passos. I had some Hemingway, but he tires me, and if we knew each other we'd have to fight. I had some Flannery O'Connor, but she makes me want to put my head in the oven. I had some Chekhov. I don't care about who's a Russky. If Chekhov's a Commie, then I wish I was one, too. But let me tell you, when it comes to writing about war, give me Stephen Crane. You can have Tolstoy. You can keep him. The son of a bitch never crossed out a sentence in his life.

I bought the typewriter with my mustering-out pay. My drafts and carbons I kept in the bottom left drawer.

One drawer was enough, because I didn't let them pile up. Every six months or so, I'd go through and read two or three pages at random of everything in the drawer, and if I didn't see anything I liked, I'd chuck them. At any given time there'd be two or three screenplays, half a dozen treatments, and one or two short stories or pieces of stories. I threw most of it away, but I did keep a log with the names of everything I'd written and who I'd sent it to, so if I ever wanted to I could see what I'd been doing for the last nine years.

I had another drink, put on a sport shirt and loafers, and went to see Mattie Reece.

Reece's office was a Quonset hut just inside the Republic studio gates. I found him where I always did, sitting behind a pair of big feet, a burning cigarette, and a pair of sharp black eyebrows. A rickety little man in a rumpled suit. He never seemed to take his feet off his desk, but somehow everything at Republic always ran smooth and tight. He could have left Poverty Row for a big job at the majors, but then he might've had to take his feet off the desk. " 'Lo, Mattie," I said.

"Hello, Ray. Come in and take a load off."

"Thanks," I said, sitting down.

"Getting a little gut there, soldier."

I shook my head.

"I can see it from here," he said.

I shook my head again. "I've had that gut for years. I don't blame you for trying to ignore it."

"Shame on you, getting out of shape like that. What if you wanted to get back in the ring?"

"I had it when I was fighting. My dance card was still pretty full. Who's this lulu you wished on me?"

"Isn't she a specimen?" he said. "I give you a week to get in. One week, you son of a bitch, if you haven't already. Tell me, how does an ugly bastard like you get in all the time?"

"A friendly smile and a firm handshake. What do you think of her?"

He opened his eyes wide. "Can you imagine posture like that on such a flimsy little thing? It's like she borrowed 'em off a fat girl." He gave a little shiver. "She wrecks me."

"Anything else?"

"Why would there be anything else?"

"She says she's being threatened."

"Ah, no," he said, concerned. "You're not coming here to ask me about her *story*, are you? The mysterious man who's gonna do mysterious bad things?"

"Sure. She's hired me to help her."

"You simple son of a bitch. I didn't give her to you to work for. I gave her to you to *boff*. I couldn't even get a glove on it, and, you know, I didn't want her going to waste."

"I already took her money."

"Yeah, well, I'm sure that'll be a novel experience for her."

"Any idea who the guy is?"

"The guy." He waved away a smell. "What makes you think there's a guy? Outside of her shaggy little head? Listen, Ray, I'm serious. You only know the girls you poke. I know every girl who ever tried to work in this town, and I'm telling you, this one's nuts. Strictly wigsville. You don't want to hop her, don't hop her, but whatever you do, don't become part of her *plans*."

"I already took her money. Who's she been hanging around with? I assume she'll simmer down and tell me, but I'd like to hear it from you."

"She don't hang, that I know of. It looks like she gave

up the starlet bit a while back. I'll give her that, she's smart enough to give up. Since then she works in stores and so forth, you know, little pretty-girl jobs. I hear she might have posed for some, ah, pictures. As for guys, she's been seen around with Lance Halliday."

"Jesus, the names out here. Who's he?"

"An 'independent producer.' Isn't that nice? He's a little hood who makes stag movies. Maybe that's what he wanted with your nut job, he heard she'd done nudie stuff. He came out here to be the new Hot Diggity, and it wasn't such a crazy idea, because he's got the face, the voice, he even moves nice, but he's one of those you get where, under the lights . . . " Mattie slowly raised his hands, wiggling his fingers. "It all fizzles away. Like ice on a radiator. He's a big blonde dreamboat and he's always got a ring on every finger. You know, the debonair Lance Halliday was in attendance, wearing his trademark rings. I guess he played around with your nut job a little, like he does with a lot of 'em, but I can't see him getting obsessed. He's too queer for himself. But no, yeah, if she bounced him hard enough I guess he could turn nasty. He's a very vain guy with not a lot to be vain about, and you don't want to kid some of those too hard."

"Could he be blackmailing her?"

"With what, for what? She's nobody."

"She says she's done stag movies. Could he be blackmailing her with that?"

"Nah. In his line of work, that's just cutting his own throat. It gets around he does that, how's he gonna get girls?"

"Where would he spend time?"

"All over. He owns part of a place called the Centaur, out in Thousand Oaks."

"I think I know it. Where does he live?"

"Palms somewhere. Come to think of it, he must have

an OK from Burri to peddle his movies."

"I thought what's-his-name ran that neighborhood. Scarpa. Lenny Scarpa."

"Sure. And Burri runs Scarpa. Wake up, beautiful. Burri runs half the West Side."

"Jesus, still? I thought he was one of those old Twenties guys."

"He ran it in the Twenties, he runs it now, he'll run it when we're both in Puppy Heaven. You want to get mixed up in something Fausto Burri's maybe part of? That what you want, Ray?"

"Listen, Mattie, I appreciate this."

"Why do I waste time on you?" Reece said without joy.

"Ah, c'mon, Mattie. Cheer up."

"Why do I waste my time?"

"I buy you drinks."

"So you say."

"C'mon, I'll buy you one now. You've done enough damage for one day."

He took his feet down off the desk one by one, like an old man, and sat there. "I hope you enjoy it when you get it," he said.

"Let's go get a drink," I said. "I just got paid."

4

Shade

In the morning I went to see the manager and squared myself on the rent. He didn't kiss me. Then I got in the car and drove over to Torrance New & Used and saw Joey Moos, who couldn't believe his luck, Ray Corson himself, right there in his own office. I'd just wanted to

get myself up to date, but on impulse I decided to pay off
the rest of the car. I liked the idea of having something no
one could take from me without stealing. It must have
been a stupid move, because it delighted Joey, and as a
token of our new friendship he tried to trade me up to a
gray '50 Merc. After that I just drove around enjoying the
sunshine. I didn't have much money left, but I owned my
car outright and I felt too good to go see Rebecca
LaFontaine. Guys probably didn't feel good around her
for very long.

She'd given me the address of a boarding house on
Flower Avenue in Venice. It was a low two-story building
with a surf shop and a hardware store on the ground floor
and, above, what once must have been a floor of cheap
offices, and of course that's where I wound up. I pushed
through a cracked plate glass door and went upstairs. The
stairs were covered with a runner of green carpet, black
and shiny with dirt and worn down to the silvery cords
underneath. They were greasy. What the hell do you have
to do to get stairs greasy? At the top was a corridor lined
with doors with pebbled glass panels, each of which was
crudely painted with a number in black, some of which
still bore old company names in flaking black paint or
gold leaf. At the end of the corridor was a Dutch door
daubed in black with the word MGR. The top half was
open. Inside, a woman in a housedress was watching TV.
She looked up at me and then back at the set.

I walked down the hall to Number 6. I couldn't make
out what had once been lettered on the glass. Someone
had scraped most of it off except for the word
APPRAISED. I knocked and heard Rebecca call, "It's
open."

There wasn't room inside for much but a bed, which
Rebecca was just then sharing with the biggest old
cowboy I'd ever seen. He had the boots, the stovepipe

jeans, the shirt with pearl snaps, and his hat was on the pillow and wasn't a disappointment. He and Rebecca were sitting side by side on the edge of the bed with a card game laid out between them. He started to get up, but Rebecca said, "Sit there and take your punishment, Lorrie. Excuse my manners, Mr. Corson, but I'm almost done giving this fellow a whuppin'."

"She is, too," he told me.

He looked like a whuppin' from Rebecca was what he'd prayed for as a child on Christmas morning.

I watched them play for a couple of minutes, each turning over the cards very intently. Finally Rebecca laid down a card and said contentedly, "That's gin. Lorrie, I'd like you to meet Ray Corson. Mr. Corson, Lorin Shade."

Shade got up at once to shake hands with me. Just when I thought he was done standing up, he'd stand up some more. He shook my hand carefully, like he'd learned that hands break easy. He had a short nose and a pocked round face, and he really was a size. I'd put roofs on smaller things than Lorin Shade. She said, "Mr. Corson and I might be doing a little business together, Lorrie. Mr. Corson used to be a boxer."

"A boxer! I like that," he said. He put up his fists, smiling, and I obligingly put up mine, and he faked a few hooks and jabs at me. I was annoyed to find I could barely keep them off me. He was fast, along with the rest of it. He dropped his hands. "I like that," he said wistfully.

"You could do the work," I told him.

I wondered what she wanted with me if she had a big boy like Shade on a string.

"Lorrie's from Warren City, Oklahoma," she said. "But he lives right down the hall. He's a stunt rider for the movies."

"Well, that's my plan," he said. "That's my long-range

plan. Right now I'm at the Ever-Brite Car Wash over on Del Amo."

"Got to start somewhere," I said.

"That's right. We're over on Del Amo, just near Anza. You keep going like you's headin' for the beach? You'll see us on the right, just before Anza. Cain't miss it. You a friend a Becky's, come by some time and I'll give you a shine. Make your car like new. On the house, if you're a friend a Becky's"

"I thought your car looked pretty nice," I told her.

"I said I couldn't afford to wash it," she said merrily. "I didn't say I wasn't washing it."

"You come on down to the car wash and I'll fix you up, too," Shade said. "Make you shine. It's right before Anza. Cain't miss it."

"Lorrie hasn't gotten his break yet, but he really is *something* in the saddle. Lorrie rides," she said sweetly and emphatically, "like a *dream*." Shade flushed with pleasure. Then he thought about it a little and began to look panicky. But Rebecca was moving smoothly onward: "He's a real ride-em cowboy. But I keep telling him, no stunt director's going to put a fellow his size on one of his horses."

"Aw, I told you, Becky," he said. "I sit real light. You know how to sit light, you can ride any size a horse."

"You did tell me that. So you did. But right now I have to talk to Mr. Corson, Lorrie. Could you be a honey right now and give us a few minutes?"

Shade stood up at once and gave my hand another careful squeeze. He told me it had been a real pleasure, and that he hoped to see me around, and maybe we could all three have us a game of poker sometime, because Becky there was quite a hand with the cards, don't think she wasn't, you might not think so but you'd be wrong, at which point Rebecca smiled at him again with almost terrifying brightness and he shut up as if he'd been kicked. "Well, so long," he said, and left, closing the door softly behind him. Rebecca smiled distractedly at the door and said, "Lorrie is the sweetest man in the world, and he's been a true friend to me. So no remarks."

"No remarks," I said.

As she had been the other day, she was dressed neatly and primly in good-quality clothes that were a little dressy for the middle of a weekday. This time it was a dark oatmeal dress, high-necked, with tiny brass buttons shaped like knots down the front and one on the cuff of each short sleeve. She took a powder-blue engagement book from her bedside table, the kind that closes with a zipper, and unzipped it. I saw she'd been using it as a notebook. What looked like a draft of a letter or an essay ran straight down the page, the words sidling around the numbers of the days like surf rolling around rocks. She opened it to a fresh page, took a pen from the little loop inside the cover, and uncapped it. Then she was ready for business. She patted the bed beside her and I sat down in Shade's place.

"I knew you'd come," she said, her eyes shining. "You have every cent I own in the world, and you could have just taken off and no one the wiser. Or you could have just laughed at me and said what money, because what proof would I have? But Mattie told me you were honest."

"Old Mattie," I said.

"I knew I picked the right man. And now I guess you deserve a little information."

"I do," I said. "First off, are we talking about Lance Halliday?"

She went completely still. She looked almost resentful. Then she leaned forward and gave me a sharp little punch in the leg. It hurt. "You've been busy," she said, beaming. "I knew I picked the right man."

"All I did was what you did," I said. "Talk to Mattie. What's Halliday been doing?"

"He's going to burn my face with lye," she said.

"Seems a perfectly nice face. What for?"

"You don't believe me."

"It's too early for believe and don't believe. Why's Halliday want to hurt you?"

"He's in love with me," she said, eyes downcast. "No, I won't use that word. He's obsessed with me. I'm, I suppose it sounds arrogant to say it, but I'm someone men get obsessed over, sometimes. Many times. I met him when I was a hat check girl at Ciro's. He's a very good-looking man, tall and very good-looking, I guess Mattie told you he was supposed to be a leading man. But I guess he was like me. He couldn't act. And he strikes everyone who meets him as awfully nice, and he was nice to me. I told him I'd have dinner with him, and then we had another dinner after that, but by then I'd found out a few things about him. He's a gangster," she said.

She said *gangster* as if it were her vocabulary word for the week.

"He makes pornographic movies," she said, "and sells them, or charges money to show them, I guess is the way it works."

"He the one you made the movies for?"

"No. Not him. And I told you, I don't ever want any more of that. Not ever. That's why it was so horrible when I found out. I didn't know if he liked me or if he was just trying to get me into one of his movies. I didn't care. I told him I didn't want to see him again. And he, he just went crazy. He just, do I have to tell you the sorts of things he said?"

"I don't know yet. You'd had two dinners?"

"I didn't sleep with him, if that's what you mean. I'm

no virgin, Mr. Corson. I suppose anyone who wanted to has a right to call me a whore. And that's why I want to get out of all this, and start over, and have a life where no one has any right to call me that."

"So he went crazy. What did you do?"

"I ran out of the place. I didn't know what to do. He'd made all sorts of threats, and I knew he was someone who could have people hurt, have anybody hurt he wanted. So I went back in, and I told him I was sorry I'd hurt him, and that I never meant to. I told him I'd stay with him all weekend and do anything he wanted, and that way he could see I was no one to be obsessed over and get me out of his system, and afterward he'd let me go. Everyone always thinks I'm going to be so wonderful, and then they find out I'm not at all. I don't ever, well, I'm just not very good. You can see I'm telling you everything, Mr. Corson."

"What did he think of your offer?"

"Oh, it was awful. It was worse than before. For a minute I almost thought he'd started beating me, hitting with his fists, but he was just talking, saying things to me I didn't think anyone could ever say to anyone. Wild things. And that's when he said about the lye. He said if I didn't want him, he'd make it so no one ever wanted me. Oh, it was horrible."

"How'd you get free?"

"I just walked out. He didn't try to stop me. I didn't know what I was doing. I felt he'd already thrown acid in my face, that he'd burned me all away. I was shaking, and on the way home I almost had a wreck."

"When did you sell him your car?"

She blinked. "That was on our first date. I told him I was worried about money, and he said I shouldn't ever have to worry about anything, and he gave me a check right then and there, and by the next time I saw him he'd talked to one of his lawyers and fixed the whole thing up. That's why I didn't go to bed with him, the first night. Because he'd just given me money."

"When was the last time you saw him?"

"Nine days ago. I spent the rest of the night just shaking, with a chair jammed under the doorknob, and the next morning I packed a bag and left. I was way up in Pasadena, in a much nicer house than this, but I thought I'd better go way across town and find someplace really cheap, because I wasn't going to go back to work either. I just never went back to Ciro's."

"What name do you use here?"

"Rebecca Stevens. Do you think that's too close?"

"No, I think that's all right. He's not going to go house to house looking for Rebeccas."

"Do you believe me a little now?"

"That about describes it. What were you thinking I could do about it?"

"Well," she said, looking happier, and set her pen to the paper. "First of all, he owns a nightclub."

"Part of one. The Centaur."

"That's right. What if you told him he'd better leave me alone, because otherwise you were going to do something to his nightclub?" As she spoke, she wrote *Threaten Nightclub* very neatly at the top of the page.

"That puts me against all his partners, too," I said. "Rebecca, unless you've got an organization, you don't threaten gangsters. That's like biting a shark. What else?"

She neatly crossed out *Threaten Nightclub*. "Well. You know the big boss of all the gangsters around there is a man named Fausto Burri. And he's supposed to be a very old-fashioned old man. What if you told Halliday that if he didn't leave me alone, you'd tell Burri that he was making pornographic movies?" She'd written: *Smut*.

"You're not serious."

She flushed. "I know my ideas probably aren't very good. I don't actually do this kind of thing, the way you probably do."

"If Halliday's making blue movies, Burri has a cut. His business is Burri's business too."

"All right, all right. But listen, what if you told Burri Halliday was going to burn me with lye? Because that's not making Burri any money. That's just a big stink for everybody, and probably bad for business, and so I suppose he wouldn't like that." She crossed out *Smut* and wrote *Bad Business*.

"You've got something there," I admitted. "Just tell Burri, and Burri would tell Halliday to lay off. Yeah, that might do it. But you don't need me for that. It's a lot better coming from you."

"I won't go to see that man," she said firmly.

"Even if it would solve your problems?"

"I won't go see him," she said, shaking her head back and forth.

"Rebecca," I said. "You're not serious. None of this is serious."

"What do you mean? I've never been so—"

"I mean you're not suggesting things you think will work. You're suggesting things you think won't work. You want me to knock your ideas down one by one until there's just one thing left to do. The one you wanted done all along."

She was silent.

"You don't really want Halliday talked to," I said. "Do you. You want him killed."

"I never said that," she said.

"It was the first thing you ever said to me."

"All right. I was being a little dramatic."

"I'm not a choirboy. But murder's a lot of trouble, and it brings a lot of trouble. Maybe we can find a smarter way. You haven't given me enough money to do murder, anyway. Or much of anything else, frankly."

"I know I haven't. I'll get you more money. That's just a first payment. I just have to think how to raise it. All I meant was, he has to leave me alone, Mr. Corson."

"Rebecca, are we going to have this witless Oh-Mister-Corson schoolgirl bit from now on? You weren't this stupid yesterday."

She smiled faintly and said, "All right, Ray, my mistake. Most men like a woman stupid." She'd been holding the engagement book like a hymnal, her knees and heels primly together, and now she eased one foot a bit backward, shifted her weight fractionally, and became the woman in the blue convertible again, wary and a bit sly.

"Maybe we do," I said, "but I can't use it now. What else do you know about Halliday?"

"I've told you what I know. I know what old movies he likes. Do you want to know what old movies he likes?"

"Not especially. Where's he from?"

"We never got to that."

"Any family here?"

"We never got to that. Do you want to hear about his old football team? Do you want to hear what he thinks of the color of my eyes?"

"What does he do for fun?"

"I think he has lots of girls. If he's serious about anyone, except, I suppose, me, he didn't say. I guess he likes a drink or two, but just like anyone else. If he drugs, I don't know about it. Look, I have a picture for you." She pulled a row of snapshots from a pocket in the back of her engagement book. It was a strip of four little pictures, the kind you get from a coin-operated photo booth, and it showed Rebecca posing with a fair-haired young man in front of a pleated gray curtain. She seemed to be sitting on his knee. In the first shot, they were displaying their right profiles together, their chins lifted. In the second, it was left profiles. In the third, they were both giving the camera sultry looks, their eyes narrowed. In the last, Halliday was lifting a hand to declaim and Rebecca was dissolving in laughter, her eyes squeezed shut and a lock of hair falling across her face and her broad, delicate mouth open. Halliday was certainly a very good-looking boy. I tucked the photos in my breast pocket and sat tapping my forefinger on my knee.

"I need a lever," I said.

"You may not find one."

"You're not too eager to see Halliday hurt, are you?"

"You didn't hear the things he said to me," she said levelly. "What he'd do, and what he'd do after that. I need to be able to walk down the street again. Ray, if your conscience won't let you do whatever this turns out to be, well, that's all very splendid, but I think I might need to talk to someone else."

"My conscience's fine," I said. "But you can talk to who you like. You want your money back?"

"You still have it?"

"No. I paid off my car with it this morning. I could get it again easy enough. Just go back and sell some of the car. You want it?"

"No. I don't. Last night I slept well for the first time since I saw Halliday. I felt I'd finally done something. I do think I picked the right man, Ray."

"I'll do what I can. Meanwhile, see about getting me some more money."

"All *right* about the money. I heard you. I'll get some money. Unless you'd rather be paid in this?" she said, flicking at one of her buttons. "I told you, it's not very good."

"I wouldn't mind finding out for myself," I said, "but whether it's good or lousy, it won't pay my rent. How about giving some to my landlord once a week?"

"How ugly a man's your landlord?"

"About like me."

"I'll get some money."

I grinned. "Better. Much better. It was a dirty crack, anyway. You're worth at least a month's rent at that dump."

"Why Mr. Corson, you say the sweetest things."

"What's Halliday's address?"

She began writing it out below *Bad Business*. "Promise," she said, "that you'll talk to me first before going over there."

"Sure, I promise. Write your phone number, too. I guess there's a phone down the hall somewhere?"

"It's not reliable, but yes." She finished writing, pulled the page from the book and handed it to me.

We stood and I looked at the page. An address, a phone number, and a row of pictures in my pocket. Nice-looking guy and his girl. And as soon as he got a clear shot, he was supposed to be throwing acid on her.

It was all thinner than tap water. It could have been true. It could have been bunkum. There wasn't any place to get a grip.

"What's wrong?" she said.

I took her by the shoulders and sat her back down on the bed. There was a straight chair by the closet, and I pulled it over and turned it around. I straddled it and sat down facing her.

"You're leaving something out," I said. "Go back to the beginning and tell it again."

5

Hat Check

The hat check room at Ciro's is shaped like an L, or so Rebecca said. The short leg of the L leads straight back from the hat check window, and they hang the coats there, near the front, because when women check furs they want to watch how you put them on the hanger. Behind the coats, you turn right and there are rows of numbered cubbyholes for the hats. When the hangers are full, you have to squeeze between the fur coats to get back there, and the coats press against you like field animals in a stall.

It was three months since Rebecca had made her second movie. By now it was out there, and somewhere men were looking at it. She knew she couldn't do that ever again, so she'd gone back to Ciro's, where she'd always had a pretty good time, but she couldn't seem to enjoy working there anymore. It was hard to stand all evening in a low-cut dress that didn't fit her, framed in the hat check window as crowds of well-dressed people went by. It was hard standing there and being looked at. It was hard to smile at men when they tipped you. She felt as if they all must have seen her movies. She felt as if she were in the stocks in the village square. There was a broken café chair at the back of the hat check room, and for ten minutes every two hours she got to sit there and rest her feet. The walls back there were unpainted, and busboys had scrawled them over with filthy drawings and suggestions, some of them mentioning her by name. She'd sit there wriggling her sore feet in her shoes and read them each over carefully, because she felt she'd lost the right to be offended by anything.

She told me she hadn't thought much of Halliday when she first saw him. He was too pretty and flashy. She assumed he was one of those young actors who liked to dress like gangsters, because he was certainly too good-looking to be anything else, and Peter Lawford had come in right behind him, and she'd wondered if they were together, but when Halliday had seen her, he'd stopped, and Lawford had gone right around him, giving Rebecca a wink as he went by. Peter Lawford was always sweet and she didn't believe the stories about him. Halliday walked up to the window, and she saw he had a ring on every finger. His blonde head was bare and he wasn't wearing a coat. Well, here it comes, she thought.

He reached into his pocket and took out a pair of sunglasses. "I'd like to check these, please," he said.

Halliday's voice didn't fit the rings or the clothes. His mouth was nice, too. He was with two other men and one of them laughed, but he didn't seem to notice. She said yes sir and hesitated, then picked up the glasses by the bridge and took them back to a cubbyhole. He thanked her when she handed him the ticket and said his name was Lance, and what was hers, and would she be on all night? She said she would. "Bad luck for you," he said. "But nice for me. Maybe I'll see you on the way out?"

"I expect you will, sir," she said.

After he went in to dinner, she went back and looked at the sunglasses sitting in the middle of the cubbyhole. They looked silly there.

She picked them up and tried them on. They were still warm from his pocket.

He and his friends came back through a little after midnight, just as the second show was starting. He said Hello Rebecca and she went back and got his sunglasses. "Can I have the ticket as a souvenir?" he asked.

The tickets were just heavy pasteboard, printed with

H. Hover Presents. You still caught hell for losing one. "Of course, sir," she said.

"It would be a better souvenir," he said, "with your phone number on it."

One of his companions laughed and was about to say something, but the blonde man looked around this time, and they all got quiet.

She agreed to meet him at Chasen's on her next night off. He'd wanted to pick her up, but she told him she always drove her own car, so if she had to she could always get in it and drive home. She was sorry, but that was her rule. He nodded and said that was sensible for a girl like her, who turned all the men into wolves. It was a slick answer but it didn't sound slick. It sounded sincere. She said, Oh, was she turning him into a wolf?

"It's touch and go," he said. "But I got willpower."

She'd always wanted to go to Chasen's and order something fancy, but afterward she couldn't say what the food was like or who was in the room, because she was falling. I asked what they talked about and she said it didn't matter what they talked about. Then she said, well, movies. They'd both thought *To Catch a Thief* was excellent. They agreed that you didn't get much better than Cary Grant. Halliday liked the way Grant was out of the cat burglar business and living in high style, but still keeping his edge. Rebecca said, what did you think about where he drops a casino chip down this French girl's front? It was awful but not the way Cary Grant did it. No one on earth wore clothes like Grace Kelly, but Rebecca didn't know why men were so wild for such an obvious iceberg. He said, we all think we're just the guy to warm her up. He said he'd been a little worried about Hitchcock after *Rear Window,* and she said what do you mean, that was a wonderful movie. She'd wanted to nurse Jimmy Stewart herself. He said Jimmy Stewart had been a sorry little punk. "Oh," she said, "so they should have cast you instead?"

"I'm not an actor," he said. "You thought I was?"

"Of course."

"Well, I guess I did, too, once. Well, what if I did? You got to take your shot."

"That's right."

"Can't just spend your life wondering. And now I don't have to wonder, and, ah, and boo hoo hoo. But it got me out of this stinking little town I come from, so I ought to be grateful."

"That's the way I look at it," she said.

"What, you too?"

"Of course me too."

"You too, huh? And they haven't given you anything? Huh. All I can say is, you couldn't be trying very hard. I've never seen a girl with more on the ball than you have. You radiate it."

"Why thank you very much I'm sure."

"I'm serious. I'd think you'd go big around here. There's a million girls in this town, but there aren't any of them like you. You couldn't really be giving it a shot. You must've just been the queen back wherever you came from."

"They fussed over me a bit," she said, "and what would you happen to know about wherever I came from?"

"Well," he said, "it's obvious."

"You mean you used to be king back wherever *you* came from."

"I don't know about king. I played some football. All right, I guess I got fussed over. You know, it was a pretty good town. I dunno why I hated it so much."

"Because they thought they owned you," she said.

"You're right. That's just what it was."

"They love you and they brag on you, and they talk

about you to each other all the time, and the more they think you're wonderful, the more they think they own you."

"I know. You can't go anywhere without hello to this one and that one, and each time they've got to make you stand there and chat and answer questions. It's not just you, of course, it's how everybody's got to talk to everybody, but you think, okay, that's another fifteen minutes of my life. And fifteen minutes and fifteen minutes and pretty soon it's seventy years and you're dead."

"They think they've got some sort of claim on you. Every last one of them."

"I swear to God, it's supposed to be only old men who think about time going by, but when I was a kid I never thought about anything else. There was this guy named Maitland who used to be the big football hero, and everybody in town could tell you every damn detail of his big touchdown against Endicott, even people who hadn't been goddamn *born* then could tell you, and we all sort of pointed him out and wasn't he great. And he was forty-five years old or something and standing behind the counter at Maitland and Son. And he was the Son, and all there was to say about him was the big game thirty years ago, and I thought, Kill me first. Just give me a rope and a chair."

"And they can't believe you don't want that too. They hate you for wanting things they don't want. When you tell them you're actually going?"

"Ah, Jesus," he said, laughing.

"You see? You know. They're all so nice, and they guess there aren't any girls in Hollywood as pretty as their little girl, and they're already proud in advance of how their hometown girl made good, but they hate you. They hate you because you're saying nothing they've got or could ever give you is good enough."

"It isn't, either. That's the sorry truth, it isn't."

"And then you get here," she said.

"Yes," he said gently, "and then you get here."

It was so wonderful, she told me, to meet someone you never had to explain anything to. Not that they didn't spend the evening explaining themselves anyway.

The only thing was, she couldn't help worrying about the expense. "What do you care about things like that?" Halliday said.

"Oh ho, Mr. Big-What-Do-You-Care. Well, I suppose I shouldn't have said anything but I can't help thinking about it. It's all very nice of you, all this. I'm afraid I'm somewhat broke."

"Broke? With a car like that?"

"I'll probably end up losing it. I can't keep up the payments."

"You shouldn't have to worry about things like that. You shouldn't ever have to worry about things."

"Well, I'm afraid I do have to worry."

He thought a moment. "How much you put in so far? You mind me asking?"

"Almost four hundred dollars. Oh, no," she said, because he was taking out his checkbook.

"Don't say no before you hear," he said, writing.

"I can't take a gift from you like that. If that's what it is."

"It's not a gift. I'm buying your car. Give me the papers when you get a chance, and I'll get it fixed for me to take over the payments."

"Well, thank you but for one thing, I need a car."

"Sure. I didn't mean for you not to have it. Look, I'm not giving you money, or even loaning you money. I'm buying a good car off you for four hundred bucks. So that's good for me. And then, since you need a car, I'm letting you borrow this car I just bought, for as long as you need. That's not such a big thing, is it? Just letting your friend borrow your car?"

"I don't know what to say."

"I know, you're thinking, okay, and what if I don't want to keep on being this guy's friend? Well, I'd be sorry about that, I'd be very sorry, but then all you'd have to do is hand over the keys and that's that. And you'd still have money in your pocket for a good used car, and some left over. See how good it is?"

He tore off the check and held it, as if it were a report card full of As and he was ready to hand it to his mother to sign and be told he was clever. He was like a kid. When she didn't reply, he got sheepish. "All right," he said, setting it down. "I guess I'm coming on a little strong. All right, I didn't mean to put you on the spot like that."

Just like a kid.

"You? Put *me* on the spot?" she said. "Little small-town hick like you? That'll be the day. Now give me my money, please," she said, and held out her hand imperiously.

He grinned and gave her the check.

"And thank you very much for the loan of your nice car."

"Don't mention it," he said.

After dinner they drove to the pier. It was his idea. He loved the boardwalk, even at night. "Look around," he said. "It's better than the zoo." They took the photo-booth strip in one of the arcades by the water. It seemed natural to sit on his knee on the little stool. They both hammed it up, making the faces they'd seen in publicity stills, and pretty soon he had her laughing too much to go on. She said, "You're funny."

"Really?" he said. "You know, I do think I'm funny. But it seems like no one else does. I guess, in my line of work, they don't call you funny much."

"What line of work's that?"

"Becky. You know what I do. I know you do. Cause all evening you haven't said, Oh, and what do *you* do? You didn't want to put me on the spot, either."

"I guess I sort of know."

"I'm a hood, all right? I can't act, but I found out there's other things I can do, and I do them. I'm one of the bad guys."

"You don't seem like a bad guy."

"Well, I am."

"Maybe I know different," she said, and put up her mouth to be kissed.

She wasn't all that good at all the other stuff, in spite of having done as much as she had, but she liked kissing. Halliday kissed very nicely. He was even gentlemanly with, maybe she shouldn't tell me this but, well, with his tongue. He waited until she finally used hers, just to let him know it was okay. Hood, she thought, kissing, hood, hood, hood. It was a ridiculous word that couldn't possibly mean anything. Not with him being so nice and so worried she wouldn't like it when he'd given her the check. She didn't even want to cash the check. She wanted to keep it. But the check was still a problem. He murmured into her ear: "Listen. Let's get into my car, and you get into my other car, and let's go someplace. Let's go home."

"No," she had to say.

She felt him go very still, then, and for just a moment, she had the idea that if she could see his face, she wouldn't like it.

But then he pulled back and looked at her, and his face was fine. "No?" he said softly.

She shook her head. "I'm sorry but not tonight. I can't tonight because you just gave me money."

"Well, I'll be— You're kidding. You can't even be *thinking* like that. A girl like you."

"You'd be surprised what I think like, a girl like me. I'm sorry. But there it is."

"Well, I'll be damned. Well. I guess that's a good one on me. You mean I wrecked it, just like that?"

She shook her head again. "I'm off again Thursday night. And maybe you could ask me out again, for then? And this time not give me any money."

"Thursday, huh? Sure. Will you go out with me Thursday?"

"I'd love to. And remember, this time, please don't give me any money."

"Ho boy. Sure. No money. I get another kiss, anyway?"

She kissed him again.

"Ho boy," he said again. "No money. Well, I'll remember."

On Thursday she put on a dress she hadn't worn for a while. When she'd first gotten to town and still had some money, she'd bought a couple of what she thought of as movie star dresses, very immodest, especially in front, but she hadn't been able to wear them since she'd made the first movie. They made her feel too much like a whore. But that night, she said, she put one on and turned in the mirror, happily. She imagined him looking at her and thinking, all for me? And then taking him home and giving him everything and making him happy. That night they went out to LaRue and he looked at her just as she'd imagined, and then they'd had a wonderful dinner and gone back to his house. His house surprised her. It was just like somebody's aunt's house, with a big flowered armchair in the middle of the front parlor. He was back in the kitchen, getting ice for their drinks, and she was wandering around the room, a little nervous so that she had to remind herself to put down her purse, and she was looking at things. There was a door to the side of the parlor, and she opened it and peeked inside

and stopped. In there was a plain-looking bedroom, and
in the corner of the room was a movie camera on a stand.
Halliday came out of the kitchen holding two drinks, saw
her standing there, and made a face. "Looking over the
old workroom, huh?"

"You make those movies," she told him.

"Sure. I told you, I'm a hood. I do lots of things.
C'mon, close the door. Let's not think about things like
that tonight."

She was shaking her head. "You make those movies."

"Rebecca," he said softly. "What? C'mon. I do worse
things'n movies. I told you."

"You didn't tell me movies."

"Well, what do you care? I'm not in them *myself*.
That's just, that's just work."

"Yes? Work? And what am I?"

He stared at her. He looked like he'd been kicked.

"What?" he said. "Aw, no. Oh, no, no, you can't be
thinking like that. Look, if I sold shoes, and I met you and
I asked you to dinner, would you say, that guy only wants
me so he can sell me a pair of shoes? That's work. You've
got nothing to do with that."

"Yes, I do. I have had to do with that. I've had everything to do with it."

He was silent.

"I'm sorry," she said.

"Well, I'm sorry, too. What do you mean, you're
sorry?"

"I'm sorry. I have to go now. I'm sorry, I can't see you
any more."

"Look, you're upset."

"I'm sorry. I have to go now. Good night. I'm sorry."

"Go? Just like that?" he said.

"Just like that," she said. "I'm sorry."

He closed his eyes then. She'd never forget it, no

matter how long she lived. He closed his eyes, and when he opened them again, they were different eyes. It was as if there was a mechanism in his head that had rolled away the old eyes and rotated a new pair into position, the same size and color as the first, but horrible. He stood there, the new eyes looking at her from inside the old face. It was the worst thing she'd ever seen.

"Enjoy the car," he said.

She just stood there, staring at the eyes.

"I must be the biggest, the biggest goddamn fool," he said quietly. "No, take the car. Take it. I'm not in the mood for it back right now."

"Okay," she said. "I'll—"

"I'll take it some other night."

"Okay," she said. "I'm sorry."

"Some night, some night when you're out riding? When you're out some night. *Miles* from anywhere," he said quietly.

She'd listened to the rest of it then, her torn stockings, her black legs and bleeding feet, and the farm hands, and how she'd love it, but by that time she'd snatched her purse up and was stumbling out the door. She slammed it and ran across the lawn and got into her car. No, it was his car now. Hood, she thought, hood hood, you can't talk like that to a hood, you can't do that to a hood, he'll kill you, I don't know what he'll do, you can't. She was holding the wheel, getting control of herself again. She told herself she had to think. She thought, You can't say you will to a hood and then you don't. All right, she told herself. All right. You have to give him what you said. You have to do what you said, she thought, the way she'd told herself when she'd first came into the room, that first room, months ago, with the man and the other man with the camera and the bed. You can do this, you've done it enough. She got out of the car again and went steadily up the walk. She rang the bell.

When he opened the door, his face looked sorry, as if it wanted to apologize. It was wet with tears, as if the eyes were hurting him, but it was the same eyes looking out as before. Still, she made herself stand there and not run. It's just him, she told herself, just him and he's upset. She said, "I'm sorry. I never meant to hurt you. I never meant to trick you. I'll stay with you tonight. I'll stay with you all weekend, just so you see, just so you know it's not that. It's that I can't be your girl. Because of the movies, but I never meant to trick you, and you can have me and get me out of your system, because you think I'm something that I'm not. I'll stay with you and you can have everything and that way you'll see I'm nothing special," and then she stopped, because he was walking toward her.

"That's nice," he said. "I can do what I want, huh? It doesn't matter to you."

She began backing away.

"It wasn't enough, I guess. It wasn't enough to string me and then turn me down. You weren't having enough fun with that. You had to come back. You had to come back and tell me I can do whatever I like and it doesn't matter. That even if I was on top of you, I'm nothing to you. You wanted to tell me with your whole body. Two evenings stringing me and laughing at me, but it wasn't enough. You had to come back and make me nothing."

She tripped and was up again in a moment, limping backward.

He said, "Fifteen minutes and fifteen minutes and fifteen minutes and then you're dead. Everybody's got to take your time. Everybody's got to make a clown of you. Tell you what we did once, though, that worked pretty good. It was this guy that was skimming on our marina operation? And we had to let everyone know, you know, that wasn't a good idea. We used lye on him, plain old lye.

On the face. You should've seen it work. It actually did
more than we planned, because it seeped down under
the lids and took one of his eyes, but that's all right, that
just made our point a little clearer, and afterward? You
wouldn't forget this guy's face if you saw it. You think I'm
kidding, or just having a little fit, or getting a kick out of
scaring you, but I'm just telling you. I'm just trying to get
a little of my time back. Maybe you're right. Maybe I'm
nothing," he said, as she reached the car and scrambled
inside. She dropped the keys and was down under the
dashboard, scrabbling for them, and his voice was
coming from above her as he stood by the car. "I must be
nothing, because you've told me it doesn't matter what I
do. But you, you're just pretty. Just a pretty face, and
without it, you're nothing, too." She sat there weeping as
the motor sawed and sawed and wouldn't catch. "I'll take
your face," he told her. "I'll make you nothing."

6

The Centaur

The first thing I did after I left Rebecca's room was call
Joan Healey down at the county courthouse. She either
worked in the probate office or with them, I kept forgetting. We didn't know each other that well anymore, but
she thought we did, and she was happy to hear from me
and promised she'd see what she could see. I said I'd take
her to lunch on Saturday and we rang off. Then I went to
the library and spent a couple hours with the atlases. I
was looking for towns named Halliday. Sometimes they'll
take their home town or their old street as a new last
name. It was a hunch I had, and after two hours I closed

the books with a list of several dozen Hallidays and
decided not to play any more hunches. I came home and
washed my new car, and poked at the right rear fender
and wondered what it would cost to have the dents ham-
mered out. It's a pretty solid car, in spite of how it looks.
Joey hadn't treated me too badly. When this one died, I'd
probably go back to him. There wasn't much in the
house, and I dumped the last of the canned hash in with
some leftover spaghetti, warmed it up in a frying pan,
and ate it.

When I finished dinner, I did the washing up.
Nothing's grimmer than coming home alone, late at
night, to a sink full of crap. My shoes needed polishing,
so I polished them, then brushed my teeth and shaved
myself twice. I spread out my suits on the bed. They're
the ones I wore bodyguarding, and neither was that good
to begin with. The brown one seemed like the better of
the two, and I put it on and had a look in the mirror. If
the light was low, I figured I could pass for an actor who
played pugs instead of a pug. I looked at the gun in the
bottom right drawer of my desk, left it there, and went
out to the car.

The Centaur was about fifteen miles out of town on
Route 5 toward the valley, a big place with a semi-
circular drive, like they've all got now. I pulled up and
gave my keys to the valet. He was a strict-looking young
Mexican. He took my keys as if all the guests drove up in
dented '41 Hudsons. My respect for the place went up a
notch, or maybe just my respect for him, and I started
down a long walkway with a line of torches on either side
that made the leaves of the shrubs gleam like metal. The
Centaur was gotten up as some sort of chateau. Beneath
the cement gewgaws, you could see it was just a big brick
shed, but they were nice gewgaws, and I passed two
doormen and walked into a foyer with a big statue of a

centaur in something that was supposed to be gilt bronze. She was rearing back on her hind legs, getting ready to wing a spear at the bandstand. She looked like she wished somebody would give her a shirt.

I walked around her rump to check my hat and had a look around. It was an enormous place. The carpeting was burgundy. Through the arch to my left I saw a row of blackjack tables and the end of what looked like a row of roulette tables, all of them well attended. Through the arch to my right was a dance floor surrounded by a horseshoe of banquettes, and behind them, a raised mezzanine with round tables and more banquettes. I wasn't the only guy there in a suit, but a dinner jacket would have been better. At the end of the dance floor sat an orchestra in gold tuxedos, making with the elbows and teeth. In front of them stood a colored girl with a mouth like a cut plum, singing very softly about something that couldn't be helped.

I went around a corner to the bar, which was of dark wood and ran lengthwise along one wall of the big room. Behind the bar was a long mirror tinted gold, and above the mirror was a long frieze in greenish glass, lit from behind. The frieze showed more girl-centaurs, hopping around with a bunch of satyrs. They didn't carry spears and looked a lot more fun to know. I ordered a gimlet and toasted them.

"Halliday in here most nights?" I asked the bartender. He was built solid, with a solid, pouchy white face.

"Friend of his?" he said.

"Admirer."

"Most nights, yeah. Fact he's overdue. You say you're not a friend of his?"

"Why?"

"In case his friends might not like you."

"Friends?"

"Always got one, two, even three guys along, and never the same ones. He must purely hate to be alone."

"Guys," I said.

"Yeh."

"Bodyguards."

"Okay," he said.

"What would one man need with so many?"

"Beats me. 'Course, if you got three, you can play a game of bridge. How's that gimlet?"

"Good," I said truthfully. "How's business?"

"We get 'em," he said. "I don't get bored. Excuse me," he said, and moved off toward a couple who'd just sat down.

He wasn't lying about business, and it was a while before he came by again. "How's that gimlet treating you?" he asked.

"I'm all right," I said. "But I'll tell you the truth. Sometimes you need a little something to pick you up. You know the feeling?"

"All the time. What can I fix you?"

"It's like I just don't have the energy any more. No zip. Sometimes I suspect I need a little something to pep me up."

"Well, that gimlet won't liven you any. Can I bring you some coffee?"

"I was thinking a little stronger."

"Something in the coffee?"

I looked him in the eye. "I just had the idea," I said, "that I might get something here to fix me up, if I asked nicely. I'd be grateful to the man who pointed the way, too."

"I can make you any kind of drink they make anywhere," he said. "I don't run a pharmacy."

"You don't run a charm school, either. You telling me all you got behind the bar's those bottles? You telling me a man can't get himself fixed up around here? Oh, now, that was unnecessary."

"What was?" he said. His face had gone very blank.

"The button under the bar. That was unnecessary." I saw two men in dinner jackets strolling toward me from the direction of the dance floor. "Here they come. How do you work it, one buzz for drunks, two for dope fiends?"

But he was busy with the cash register and couldn't hear me.

One of the dinner jackets was a pretty little fellow, a real pocket edition. But I've known some pocket editions and I wasn't giggling. The other was more of a size. Neither was young. The small one said, "Mr. Burri sends you his compliments, sir, and wonders if you might join him at his table."

I'd seen Fausto Burri in the papers. His table was by the dance floor, with a view of the front entrance. He was a narrow man who could have been fifty, though I knew he must have been over seventy, with a dark, heavily creased face, a weak jaw, and a strong nose. He wore a snowy white shirt, a dark red tie figured in dull silver, and a quiet charcoal suit that must have cost more than any car I've ever owned. His suit was what my suit wanted to be when it grew up. My suit was kidding itself. "Good evening, Mr. Burri," I said as they walked me up to him. "My name's Ray Corson. What can I do for you?"

He said, "Please, Mr. Corson, sit, sit."

"Thanks." I sat. At his elbow was a glass full of some clear liquid and a little dish of chalky-looking little cookies. He looked at my empty hands and said, "You don't have your drink."

"That's all right," I said.

"Excuse me, please, it's not. This is not a place, a man comes here for a drink and they don't let him drink it."

He was looking toward the bar, and now he moved his chin fractionally in my direction. He settled back. "That kind of place we don't run. Tell me, you like our little place?"

"It's quite an operation, sir."

"Ah. You don't like my place."

"I'm afraid it's not the kind of place I'm used to."

"No? Well. I'll tell you something." He leaned closer. "It's not my kind of place, either. Ah? That surprises you? It's true."

"Why not?" I said.

"Look around," he said. "These people."

"They look all right to me."

"Sure, all these highly desirable customers with the money they got. You know what I call them? I call them lowlifes. Their money, they don't work for it, they just got it. Like a rash. What good's it do 'em? I don't know. Here they are every night, the men like fairies and the women naked, just naked. Okay, it's about time."

A slim brunette with a neck like a gazelle had appeared at my shoulder, wearing about as much cloth of gold as you'd need to keep the chill off a canary. She set a fresh gimlet in front of me as if she were kissing her baby goodnight. Burri watched me taste it and looked pleased when I nodded. It was as good as the first.

"Here they are, every night," he continued. "And they drink, not a nice civilized drink like we're having together here, but I think you could say they guzzle, and they stuff themselves, and what they put in their mouths I wouldn't touch with my hand. The food here, I'm sorry to say it, I wouldn't touch it with my bare hand. They call it French. They got to have the French food, and the booze, and the roulette, and the naked women, and they—" He held a thumbnail under his nose and gave a delicate sniff. "But what can I say?" he said, extending his hands and looking surprised. "Life is difficult. Very painful, and people need to have a good time. And maybe I don't like their good time or their music, *but*, I happen to be in that business. Of helping people enjoy themselves. And it's not such a bad business."

"Yes, sir."

"Now, your business I don't know. This," he said, holding the thumb beneath his dark nose again, "this interests you?"

"I'm interested in anything that'll turn a profit and not cause too much fuss."

"That, young man, is a very wholesome and sensible attitude. It is my own attitude. A little profit, and not cause a fuss, but it's very easy to remember the profit and forget the no fuss. You were causing a little fuss at my bar, anh?"

"I didn't mean to."

"You wanted to know, will my man there sell you a little something."

"I wanted to know if that kind of thing could be gotten here."

"Ah. Because you're in that business? You see I'm asking you very politely."

"I do, sir. Right now I'm not in any business at all. I guess you could say I've had an offer."

"And this man who's offering— I'm being very patient. This man is who? In which business?"

"I'd rather not say, sir. He was candid with me, and we may work together, and he deserves a certain amount of discretion."

"You'd rather not say."

"I'm afraid not."

"You'd rather not say."

"I'm sorry."

"I couldn't persuade you?"

I looked from the little gunman to the big one. "With both your boys working? Yeah. But it would take a while, and you couldn't do it here."

"Now," he said cozily, "this is nice. Keeping the mouth shut, this is something not everybody understands. Very admirable, *if* your business is not my business. *But*. What if your business is my business after all?"

"Then I'm out of that business. That's why I came here."

"You gotta speak slow for an old man. You came to find out, is it okay."

"Yes."

"This mysterious business."

"That's right."

"With Mr. Halliday."

"I don't think I mentioned a name."

"That's very true. I must be making a mistake."

"Isn't Lance Halliday a partner of yours?"

Burri pursed his lips and raised his eyebrows. "I must admit to you now, I never heard him referred to like that before."

"I mean a partner in this club."

"Oh. Yeah, we gave Mr. Halliday a little interest in our undertaking."

"I heard him described as the club's owner," I said, smiling faintly.

"People talk," Burri said sadly. "You've nearly finished your drink. Now, this time I truly hope— Ah. No. Here it comes." The gazelle reappeared at a canter, looking a bit alarmed, and set down another gimlet in front of me. As she was about to leave, Burri lay a brown hand on her bare back. "Young lady," he said.

"Yes Mr. Burri," she said tensely.

"You are taking very nice care of us, young lady."

"Thank you Mr. Burri," she said. He lifted his hand

and watched fondly as she walked on taut legs back to the bar with her tray against her hip. The tray covered more of her than the dress did.

"They're a regular plague, these naked women," I agreed.

Burri and his torpedos all turned to look at me at once.

Then Burri smiled, showing a beautiful set of false teeth. "Mr. Corson. I gotta admit. You seem to have your wits about you, but at the same time you are not what I would call a nervous gentleman." I smiled back and said nothing. "Mr. Grasso," he said, "what do you think of Mr. Corson here?"

"You never can tell," the little gunman said judiciously.

"Big one," offered the big one.

"Mr. Corson, if you weren't so busy with your mysterious friend, I might even think of something to discuss with a capable young man like yourself."

"Thanks, Mr. Burri. But I should warn you, I'm not Sicilian."

He chuckled. "Sicilian I don't care so much anymore. I'm not old-fashioned. I'll do business with any man if he's a gentleman and can make me a nice proposition. I'll do business with a nigger. I got a Negro gentleman works for me and he is a fine gentleman. His name is Hubie Howard the bandleader, and I must admit he has my admiration as a businessman. Because here is a man who works with animals, with *animals*— and yet, there's never a problem, and things are always very orderly with Mr. Howard, and he gives me my nice music, all right, it's not nice music, but it's the kind you got to have and he gives it to me with no fuss. And this interests me very much. Because this colored fellow is solving the identical, exact same problem I got myself every day."

"Of working with animals," I said.

"Animals," he said. "People who got ambition and

that's all they got. People with no discipline, who don't know to ask, Is this okay. And these are not people you can reside your trust in. They are people you always got to be watching. And you know, nothing so very nice happens to these people in the end."

There must have been some signal I missed, because the big pug was standing and lifting away Burri's table, and Burri started getting up on his long rickety legs. I stood too, and Burri gave me his hand to shake. It was cool and dry. "Mr. Corson, you strike me as a fine young gentleman, and I'd like you to have a good time tonight at the bar with the compliments of the house. And maybe some evening you'll come by again and we'll have another nice talk."

"I'd like that," I said.

"And about our friend," he said. "So you know. Our friend has an okay to do a few little things. But if you are interested in this,"—he displayed his thumb again—"this is not a good business to be in with him."

"But it is a good business to be in with you?"

"Ah ha hah!" he said, waggling a finger at me. "Now I see. *Now* I see. You want your mouth shut and my mouth open, anh?" Laughing merrily, he turned and swayed off on his long legs, a gunman on either side.

I sipped my drink and watched him go. The gazelle reappeared to take Burri's glass and dish of cookies. She smiled and asked if I needed anything else. It was a friendly smile, but it did convey that just because I was Mister Burri's new friend didn't mean I could go sitting in Mister Burri's booth when he wasn't there. I drained my drink, set the glass on her tray with a dollar, and went back to the bar. By the time I got there, the bartender had another gimlet waiting. I'd be doing well to get home that night with my liver still attached.

I sat down, saying, "For a minute back there, you

seemed to forget all about me. I was lonely."

"Friend," he said. "I don't know what the hell you're doing. But you know what I'm doing. I'm working for a living."

"I didn't take it personally."

"I wouldn't care if you did. Actually, though, now you're part of the family, I guess I got to care. What's your magic, anyway? I never seen the old man fall in love so fast."

"You pour a good drink," I told him.

"Thanks. That's one thing here, they let you pour 'em right. It's why I've stayed so long."

"Thinking of going?"

"Been saving up for my own place. Another year should do it. I got my eye on a property in Culver City."

"Yeah? Which? If you're behind the bar, I'll have to make a note of it."

"Friend, don't take this wrong, especially since you're Burri's new nephew. But when I get my place? I don't want you anywhere near it."

I left him with a smile and no tip and went to get my hat back. Outside, I gave my ticket to the valet. He still treated me like I didn't smell, and I gave him two bucks, his and the bartender's, and pulled out the circular drive and headed north. A quarter mile up the road, I made a U-turn and drove back. There was a liquor store, a florist, and a late-night drugstore across the road from the Centaur, and I pulled into the parking lot, where I could see the club's entrance, and killed the lights. They might have a man watching the road, just on general principles, but unless he was on the roof with binoculars I didn't see where they could put him, and I figured I was probably clear.

My watch said about 9:40. I decided I'd wait an hour to see if Halliday showed. They had strong lights under the port cochère, I'd seen his picture, and there's nothing wrong with my eyes. In the army, I was company sniper. It's interesting what snipers do. When your company retreats, you're supposed to cover them by climbing a tree or something and firing on the approaching enemy. They don't say what you're supposed to do when the Germans arrive and you're still up the tree. I didn't mind. By the time I joined up I was twenty-six and had been on the bum for eight years, just rattling around loose from town to town, and I was ready for someone to tell me what to do, even if they were telling me to go climb a tree and wait to be shot. Anyway, we didn't retreat much and I made it to the Elbe without so much as a skinned knee. Around ten past, a dark blue Lincoln pulled up with two suits in front and a blonde head in back. The blonde head got out and became a big young guy with sort of sparkly hands and what looked like Halliday's chin. He breezed right by the valets with his hard boys and breezed back out at 10:25. By then I had my engine running, and I slipped into traffic two cars behind him.

7

Jade Mountain

We headed back toward town on the Golden State. The radio was broken, so I was singing *That's Amore*. I had the window open and was letting my hand fill with cool wind and molding it like clay. Late as it was, there was a bar of dull blue light floating over the western horizon somehow, and the glow you always see over downtown, and all the lights, spreading out to the mountains. When they turned east onto 10 I was right behind them, and a

good thing, too, because they turned off right away onto
Soto and if I'd been bashful I'd have lost them. We
cruised through Boyle Heights for a few blocks and then
they pulled into a big Chinese place called Jade
Mountain. I pulled into a supermarket two blocks further
on, got the car turned around, and waited.

The market had a big neon sign of a performing seal.
It had a red ball balanced on its nose, and then the ball
was floating a little above its nose, and then higher, and
then gone. Then it reappeared on the nose again. After
five minutes I drove back to the Jade Mountain. The blue
Lincoln was in the back corner of the lot, almost out of
sight behind the restaurant. I got out of the car, locked
my door, and went inside.

The bar was off to the right as you come in the front
door, one of those grotto things with a low ceiling, all the
light coming from behind the bottles. There was an old
Chinese gent in a short jacket behind it, and Halliday at
the far end, chatting with the cocktail waitress. She wore
a snug brocade dress and had a smooth cool face you
wanted to cup in your hands. Her waist was about as big
as my neck. He had big rings on every finger, as advertised. They must have been pure hell during piano
lessons.

I guessed his lugs were still out in the car. Aside from
us, the bar was empty. I sat down at the other end and
ordered my fifth gimlet. I hoped there weren't going to
be too many more. The waitress was neat and smooth.
She had everything a man could want, only little. She and
Halliday looked awfully pretty together, and I watched
them talk and tried not to get sad. People talk a lot of
crap about the Chinese being inscrutable, but there was
nothing mysterious there. She was looking up at him as if
she thought he was just fine. He gave her a business card,
and she did a little series of head-bobs over it and

admired it and tucked it away somewhere in her dress. Then he kept talking, looking friendly and reasonable, and you could see her wondering if she might not be understanding him right. Then her face went slowly dead, and then she said something brief and walked steadily out of the bar. Halliday looked after her ruefully. When he turned, he found me grinning at him. I raised my glass.

He came over in no hurry and said, "Laughing at me, friend?" It was a nice voice, medium deep and not trying too hard.

I shook my head, still grinning. "Toasting you. You got more nerve than I do."

"For whatever good it did," he said, sitting down next to me. "I guess I got told."

"I guess. What were you told?"

"Actually, I couldn't make it out. But whatever it was, I got told, all right."

"Honorable wound, anyway. Let me buy you a drink. Make up for my bad manners."

"The hell you'll buy me a drink," he said amiably. "I just got trimmed down to nothing. I need to feel like a big shot again. I'll buy."

Halliday was about the best-looking man I've seen. He had thick, dull blonde hair swept straight back from a broad forehead, thick straight brows, a straight nose that wasn't too small, and a small, sensible-looking mouth. He might've had a little more jaw than he needed, but it had a good shape. He wore a tan mohair jacket with shoulders padded out to here, but he had plenty of his own shoulders underneath. He wasn't sissy-looking, either, like some of these perfect types. His eyes were calm and he looked friendly. You found yourself thinking it wasn't his fault he was gorgeous. You almost thought the rings weren't his fault, either.

He asked me my name and I told him Stuart Rose, and we shook hands. I don't look much like a Yid, but neither did Rosey. We'd gotten to be pretty good friends at Camp Claiborne and stayed that way until halfway through the Ardennes. He wouldn't have minded me using his name. He didn't need it anymore. Halliday told me his name was Halliday and I said "Huh."

"Heard of me?" he said.

I said, "Director, right?"

"More of a producer."

"You thought little Lotus Blossom was your next big star?"

"That's right."

"Must be the only woman in L.A. who doesn't want to be in the movies."

"Well," he said lightly, "maybe she doesn't like the kind of movies I make."

"What kind are those?"

"Well, you know. We strive to entertain."

"Guy with your looks, how come you're not in front of the camera instead?"

"Tried it," he said. "Stank up the joint. Now I produce."

"Landed on your feet, huh?"

"Hope so, anyway. You look like you might've played a little ball sometime."

I shook my head. "I come from a pretty small town, and pretty much all the guys were on all the teams. But I never cared for it much."

"I was a tailback," he said. "I wasn't bad, either. I could hit a little and run a lot, and we had a quarterback with an arm and some guys on the line who could chase off the riff-raff. We did all right. That was a good time. That was about as good a time as I've had. Of course, when I was acting, my press bio said I was the quarterback."

"Where was this?"

He shook his head. "I'm funny about that, I guess. I'd rather not say."

"Ashamed of your old home town?"

"Other way round, friend," he said. "Other way round. I don't think everybody there would be too pleased with some of the things I've done out here. I guess it doesn't matter anyway, but like I said, I'm funny about it. Anyway, the press kit said Tarzana, which sounds better than the real thing would've, anyhow."

"Quarterback from Tarzana."

He grinned. "I wouldn't've been quarterback, even if I'd had the arm. I was having too much fun where I was. You never played football? You must've done something. I don't meet that many guys who make me look dainty."

"Boxed a little."

"Yeah? Pro?"

"For a while. Army and then pro."

"Kid Rose, huh?"

I laughed. "I was thirty when I had my first professional bout. I fought as plain old Stu Rose."

"How'd you do?"

"Nine and two. Six of the nine were knockouts or TKOs, most of them in the first three rounds. That's not bragging. That's to say I couldn't box. I could hit, but that's all. If you made me box, you could take me on points. I quit before everybody knew it."

"You must've been able to take a punch, then, too."

"I don't like it, but I don't mind it."

"Didn't, or don't?"

"What are we talking about?" I said.

The waitress came back and dropped Halliday's business card on the table. She turned on her heel and walked off without a word. Halliday looked at me with raised eyebrows, then picked up the card and turned it over. On the back, there was a phone number in a neat feminine hand and a deft little sketch of a movie screen with a smiling, almond-eyed face on it. I gawped at it with my jaw hanging down. The thing about me is, I really understand women.

Halliday laughed. "Don't feel too bad. I thought just what you thought: not a chance." He tucked the card away. "You say you boxed in the Army? This Korea?"

"Flatterer," I said. "Belgium and Germany, and I was pretty old for that."

"Siegfried Line, huh? I guess you saw some action."

"It got a little noisy."

"How was that?"

"Well, I don't like it when people shoot at me. But they gave me a gun to shoot back with, so I guess it was okay."

"Combat didn't bother you any?"

"Sure. But it was better than sitting around. When you're mixing it up, you're too busy to get scared. When you're lying around waiting, you've got nothing to do but picture different ways you could get it."

"What was the worst thing you ever saw?"

"Out there? I dunno. I never tried stacking 'em up against each other."

"Tell you what I mean," Halliday said, turning his glass around bit by bit as if he was looking for something along the outside of it. "There are some things you see, they get under your skin like a splinter and just stick. You keep seeing them. Give you an example. When I was a kid, I had this sort of gang I ran with. I guess I was the leader, or anyway, the guy who always had an idea what we could do next. And there was one of these jerky little guys who used to try and run with us. You know the type. Funny-looking and never does anything quite right. We used to give him a pretty bad time. Anyway. One day we were all out somewhere north of town, and I noticed these three trees next to each other that had big branches pretty much at a level. And I said, I'm going to climb up that tree over there, and walk across the branches on *that* tree in the middle, and not climb down until I'm on *that* tree. So I did, and of course, then everybody had to try. We were all crazy for something to do. Well, some of the kids made it fine, and some chickened out partway and had to crouch down and wriggle back, and some decided they'd better stay on the ground. But Gavin, that was the kid's name, Gavin was hell-bent to show he could do it, and halfway across he dropped like a stone, maybe fifteen feet, and broke his arm, the compound kind. Where there's a little nub of bone poking out."

"Well, there you go," I said.

"No, wait. He broke his arm, and it was the best thing ever happened to him. We carried him back to town, even though we shouldn't have, and he didn't make a noise practically the whole way. When he was in the hospital, we all came to see him. It was more attention than he ever had in his life. And when he got out, he was one of us. Everybody just agreed that, without talking about it. And once he was in, you know? He wasn't so jerky. He was pretty much one of the fellows from then on. He got what he'd wanted. But you know, not a week probably goes by that I don't see that little nub of bone in my mind, and I'm not squeamish. I just think about Gavin wanting so badly to be one of the guys. And then him lying there with his bones poking out. And it seems as if, whenever things are going along nice and smooth, I'll always see that sharp little nub again, and it—" He made a hooking gesture with two fingers. "*Catches.*"

"Huh," I said.

"Well, that's the sort of thing I'm talking about," he said.

"That's a good story."

"Your turn."

"Huh. All right. Well, I guess a lot of things over there happened that stuck with me. But what I think you're talking about, that one's just something I saw for thirty seconds out the back of a truck. It was just a guy slapping a woman around."

"That's what you remember, huh?"

"I know. We saw a lot of things out there. There were these things called tree-bursts, where the Germans wired a charge to a tree as they were retreating, head-high or knee-high or, you know, balls-high, and I saw one of those take a man's head off who'd just been humping along next to me singing Bang Bang Lucy. And there were towns we came through that you could tell had been beautiful, and now they were just a few stone walls and a big sea of trash. And we'd done that. Helped, anyway. But the kind of thing you're talking about?" I took another swallow of my drink. "I remember this guy. I didn't know his name, but he was in our company. We were rotating to the front after ten days back, and everybody was stopping overnight in a place called Vise, in Belgium, and trucks'd been coming in all day. And I guess this guy had gotten himself a Belgian girl, but he wasn't pleased with her. He had her by the arm, even though she wasn't trying to go anywhere, and he was slapping away with his free hand, grinning down at her. He'd stop and wait for her to lift her head, and then give her another one. He was enjoying himself. I guess he was pretty lit up."

"And that stayed with you."

"I know, it was just a few slaps. He wasn't even closing his fist."

"But it stayed with you."

"I'm not getting to the point of this. They were

feeding us good. They were treating us all right. He didn't have any call to act that way. I don't care how drunk he was. But that isn't it, either. It's the way she was standing there taking it. Like everybody had a perfect right to step up and do whatever they liked to her. Like that's what she was born for. You know what I'm talking about."

"Sure," he said. "Gavin."

"That's right, Gavin. No one's got a right to lean on somebody like that, who can't help themselves, who can't even cover up, because they think they must deserve it."

"All right, Rose," he said mildly. "We were just kids."

"It's not just kids. Everybody does. Everybody. I'll never forget it, any part of it. She'd curled her hair, and now it was all down over her face, and she wasn't a beauty, and she was wearing man's shoes too big for her. His blouse was coming untucked over his hip. The guy next to me in the truck was eating an orange, and he'd just given me some, and my fingers were wet with it. And this man was whaling on this woman who'd been born to take it. I'd seen it all my life, but just then's when I realized, I'd always be seeing it. Because that was the world."

I took a breath and finally managed to shut up. Halliday had something, all right. You wanted to talk to him.

He waited a minute, then said, "What did you do?"

"What do you mean?"

"What did you do to the guy when you found him?" Halliday said.

I didn't say anything.

"Okay. Fair enough," he said. "We just met."

At last I said, "I didn't do anything he wouldn't get better from someday."

"Galahad, huh?" he said lightly.

"No," I said slowly. "I'm not a Galahad. I'm a bully,

too. I guess that's why I hate 'em so much."

After a moment, he laughed.

It was pretty nice of him, actually. He knew what I was talking about. But we just sat there laughing, like I'd been joking.

"Listen, Rose," he said when he'd stopped. "Tell me something. What sort of things scare you?"

"What? Jesus, I don't know. Lots of things. I'm not stupid."

"What kinds of things?"

"Your little Lotus Blossom, like I said."

He laughed. "Wise man. Me too, boy. Ever hear of a guy named Lenny Scarpa?"

"Sure."

"He make you nervous?"

"He's just a guy."

"Who can kill you."

"Anyone can kill you, if you let them. What are we talking about here?"

"What are you doing with yourself these days?"

"Not enough. I work construction when I can."

"And?"

"I've done a little bodyguarding. What are we talking about?"

"A little bodyguarding, maybe, to start. I don't know. I'm thinking it through. I might be able to use a guy like you in my business."

"The movie business," I said.

"I think you know what kind of movies I make," he said.

"I guess I do. Much money in that?"

"Enough," he said. "Worried about your pay?"

"Not yet," I said. "Sounds like an entertaining business. What other lines of work you in?"

"Why should there be anything else?" he said.

"I dunno. I guess some movie producers hire body-guards. I was just wondering if the movies was all there was."

"Doesn't seem like enough?" he asked softly.

I said, "I just wanted to know what my duties might be. Am I just protecting you from irate older brothers, or was there something else you needed done?"

For some reason, he didn't like that at all.

He didn't close his eyes, like Rebecca said he had, but they changed, all right. I saw a little light come on way back in them, like the pilot light in an oven.

"You worry about the little sisters, champ?" he said.

It was still a nice voice, but now it didn't match the eyes. Maybe it wasn't so nice.

"I don't worry much," I said. "I thought it was a pretty simple question."

"Maybe you're a bit of a Galahad after all. Is that it?"

"If we're going to work together, I ought to know something about the business."

"We weren't talking about working together, champ. We were talking about you working for me. Right now I don't think we're talking about anything."

"And a minute ago you were full of charm," I said sadly.

"I'm still full of charm, champ. Maybe I spread it around too thick. Maybe you've already had your share."

"Maybe I could get tired of hearing you decide what my share is."

"I don't think I can use you after all," Halliday said. "I don't really have a spot right now for someone with your manners."

The hell, it was over now.

I said, "When I need lessons in manners, junior, I won't come to you. And don't think you can give me one on the house. You're better at running than hitting, remember?"

Halliday nodded slowly, then got up. There's not many people who can get up off a barstool and look graceful, but he did, sliding the stool gently out of the way behind him with one foot as he went, so he wouldn't have to bump into it or edge around it. It didn't seem like a performance, especially, or any more of one than everything else he'd done. He had both hands on the bar, so that his rings made one glittering row, and he looked at them for a moment. He nodded to himself.

"I guess that concludes our program for tonight," he said.

He got out his wallet and dropped some money on the bar.

"See you, Halliday," I said. "Thanks for the drink."

"Don't mention it," he said, looking past me. "So long."

"So long," I said.

He walked down to the end of the bar. There was a side door there that led out to the parking lot, and he went out and closed it behind him.

I sat there and finished my drink. I was pretty hot with myself. I'd pushed in too fast and then lost my temper. I ought to have myself under better control than I do. Well, five gimlets. But Jesus, whose cheap date was I that I had to drink them? I guessed it was worth something to have seen that little light in his eyes. To know it was there. It made it that much easier to buy Rebecca's story. He could get mean, or anyway, look like it. And he could control it better than I do. What else? He didn't like people thinking he was small-time. Who does? There was something else there, too, about when I'd asked what he wanted me for. But it'd gone by too fast. He was hung up about combat. So are a lot of guys who haven't seen any. He was pretty bright. Pretty sensitive, for a hood. He thought he was some kind of amateur shrink. So do a lot of people in L.A.. He knew how to get off a barstool without snagging his nylons. I counted the money on the bar. Whatever else he was, he wasn't a piker. I sighed, shoved my chair back, and headed for the door to the parking lot.

When I got outside, I saw Halliday sitting alone in his car across the lot, the motor running, and two guys in suits standing to my right. I kept walking. Halliday nodded pleasantly and started backing out toward the exit, his elbow on the edge of the open window and his forefinger resting on the top of the side mirror, and the two men in suits stepped in close. One of them wore a watch that was big even for him, with dials and knobs all over it, and the other one had clear brown eyes and the kind of shaped mouth that made you want to trust him. The one with the big watch put a hand on my chest, and I stopped and looked down at it.

"That's a mistake," I said. "Undo it."

"We need to talk a minute, Mr. Rose," he said.

"You don't look like much of a conversationalist. Take that hand away."

"Listen, friend," he said. "We need to talk about how you talk to people."

I knocked his hand off.

He leaned in and took hold of my necktie. He got some collar, too. "Listen," he said.

Maybe it's because I was such a lousy boxer, but I don't see the point of going move and countermove with people who ought to know the moves as well as you do. What I'd rather do is upset the board. I gave out a sort of groan and began to sit down, as if I were tired or having an attack, and without thinking the pug tried to pull me

back up again by the tie. All two hundred forty-odd
pounds of me, one-handed. I almost felt sorry for him.
But by that time it was out of my hands, or anyhow, like
I've said, that's what I always tell myself, and I came up
again fast, grabbing the back of his neck as I went, and
broke his nose with my forehead. The pug fell back
clutching his face and screaming way back in his throat,
and his buddy moved in, but glancing over at his friend
instead of tending to business, and I kicked out sideways
and broke the buddy's knee. That would have settled me
for a while, but he looked like he wanted to get up again
somehow, and I kicked him in the belly, which made him
more introspective. By this time the first guy had gotten
out his gun and lit off a couple, clutching his face and
firing half-blind. That was just plain bad taste. When
you're close enough, you treat a gun like you'd treat a
right hook: if you can't shrug it off, you get inside it. I got
inside and yanked his arm the way it was already going
and gave him a couple of elbows in the body as he went
past, then brought my elbow down on his collarbone
when I had a chance. It dropped him on his belly. I
stamped on the back of his head and he let go the gun. I
dragged him backward until his gun hand was trailing
half off the curb of the sidewalk, and then I stamped on
his knuckles and felt them go. I stamped again on his fin-
gertips, hoping to get the thumb, or at least break some
of his fingers twice, and then I felt something move by
my ear and heard a shot from a .38. I stopped.

"You goddamn psycho," said the guy with the knee.
He was down on one elbow with his gun leveled at my
chest. "Don't you move. Don't you move a lick. I put 'em
where I want 'em, and the next one's yours."

He had the floor.

"You goddamn psycho. What's the matter with a guy
like you? What's the matter? We weren't supposed to kill

you. We weren't even supposed to mark you. We were just told to give you a shove and a warning, and look. Look what you turn it into."

"He threw down on me," I said.

"None of this had to happen."

"He threw down on me," I said. "Next time he'll have to do it lefty."

"You're a goddamn psycho. I had a dog like you, I'd have it put down. The only reason you're living is, Halliday wouldn't like I killed someone he didn't say to. You come at him again, or me, and I'll forget what Halliday wouldn't like. Now get going."

I let him have the curtain line. He hadn't said anything inaccurate. His colleague was still out, making wet snoring noises. I turned and headed back for my car. In front of the entryway, I saw what looked like a little brocade package on the sidewalk. Lotus Blossom had run out when she heard the shots, hadn't liked what she'd seen, and had hunkered down hugging her legs, her head tucked against her knees. As my footsteps came closer, her head came up slowly, like someone was pulling it up on a string. Her shiny black eyes were the size of hubcaps, and her mouth was open.

"I think your right profile's your best," I said as I went by.

8

Scarpa

I had a card for an after-hours place in Gardena, and I went there and stayed until past three, drinking and trying to cool down. I was still asleep next morning when

someone started hammering on my front door. I opened
my eyes and watched the knob shiver. I was too tired to
swear. The drapes were shut. A smart guy, even a half-
smart guy, would have pretended nobody was home. I
pulled on some pajama pants and opened the door. Two
neatly dressed men with guns backed me smoothly into
the room. Neither of them stood higher than my chin,
but they didn't seem to have a complex about it. One had
a very round head and the other had light green eyes with
rusty brown hair, the kind that makes ridges. Aside from
that, they were nondescript, the way men like that ought
to be. "Someone wants to talk to you," the round-headed
one said, almost pleasantly. "Let's go."

I stood there scratching my belly and staring. Then I
turned around and walked back to my bed. "Nuts," I said,
climbing in. "You didn't come to shoot me, or it'd be
done. So you must want to tell me something or ask me
something. Either way, I can hear you from here."

I closed my eyes.

"They told us you were a cutie," the green-eyed one
said. "I guess we were warned."

"If you came here to tell me I'm cute, consider me
told. Close the door on your way out, and tell your boss
I'm tired of waltzing with his punks."

"We're not Halliday's boys," the round headed one
said. "We're not as easy as Halliday's boys. C'mon,
let's go."

I fixed up the pillow again and got comfortable.

"You know your problem?" Round Head said. "One of
'em? You make more of things than you oughta. My guess
is, what we're discussing here? Is ten minutes of conversation. No lie. You could be back in your own little bed
while the blankets're still warm." I heard him hit a few
licks at random on my typewriter.

"Don't do that with no paper in," I told him, opening

my eyes. "It's bad for the platen."

"I know," he said. "I'm always after my kids to quit monkeying around with ours." He picked the typewriter up one-handed by the frame, swung it around, and held it out at arm's length. The floor was linoleum over concrete slab. No give. Ten bucks would've bought me another typewriter just as good, but this was the one I'd used to write everything I'd ever tried to write. And I didn't have ten bucks to spare. I climbed back out of bed and said, "Let me get some clothes on."

"You're beautiful just the way you are," he said. "Let's go."

Green Eyes walked beside me and Round Head followed behind as I slopped out the front door and past the office to the parking lot, barefoot and naked except for a pair of old pajama bottoms. It was a pretty day. I had that feeling in my gut you have when somebody's about to do something, maybe you, maybe not. There was a long cream Caddy in the lot, the windows tinted almost black. Green Eyes opened the door and I climbed inside. Through the murk I could see Round Head leaning back over the front seat, tracking me with his gun. The man in the back seat was about thirty-five, a solid, compactly made man whose face didn't fit. It was narrow and all jaw. You could have plowed the North Forty with it. He wore a sharkskin suit with lapels that were almost too wide, but not quite, and a look of mild disbelief that seemed to be permanent. The door thudded shut behind me and the Caddy eased away from the curb and slipped into traffic like it was slipping into a warm bath. The man said, "What happened last night at the Jade Mountain?"

I said, "What makes it your business?"

The look of mild disbelief didn't change. "You know who I am?"

"No."

"I'm Lenny Scarpa."

"Okay, I know who you are. Everybody says the nicest things about you, too."

"What happened last night?"

"What the hell makes it your business?" I said. "You drag me out of my bed, eight in the morning, the head nun come to spank me with a ruler. C'mon, buddy, youse are goin' fer a ride. Jesus, you must love old movies. Ask me a civil question and I might answer it, but right now? I've got no reason in the world to talk to you."

Scarpa glanced at Round Head, amused.

"What," I said, "the gun? What good's the gun? All you can do with it is shoot me or club me, and either way, your question goes unanswered."

"You think I couldn't make you sorry?"

"If you're Lenny Scarpa, I hope to God you got better things to do than ride around Hawthorne making me sorry."

"These guys," he told the roof of the car. "There's a place someplace, and out comes these guys, and they come to me."

He began to laugh.

"*Mister* Corson," he said. "It's *so* good to have you with us this morning. My name is Leonard Scarpa. I hope we haven't caused you no inconvenience?"

"Not at all, my son," I said. "And what can I do for you today?"

"What the goddamn happened at Jade Mountain?"

"Job interview."

"Take him someplace and hurt him," he told Round Head.

"That's the house number," I said, grinning. "Why wouldn't it be? Halliday thought he could maybe use me. My own manners must've been poor. He told his punks to lean on me. I leaned back."

"You tailed him there from the Centaur."

"I wasn't going to make my play in front of a room full of people who think he's an independent producer."

"Why would you want to work for him?"

"I need a job."

"It adds up," he admitted. "You're just the kind of Mau-Mau Halliday likes. Wild. No control. You know, those guys, they're both still in County General, and one of 'em's prob'ly ruined." He sat there, thinking it over. He gave me the look while he was at it. He did it pretty well. I still thought I should be getting a professional discount. Then he fished in his breast pocket, brought out a deck of cards, and shuffled them expertly without looking. He fanned them and held them out to me.

It was a Tarot deck. The card I picked showed a man standing on one foot in front of a tree. Then I saw I had it wrong way up. The man was dangling head-down from a branch by a rope around his ankle, his hands tied behind his back. He looked like he wanted to go back a few bars and take it from the bridge. "That's your significator," Scarpa said. "The Hanged Man, reversed. Huh. I would've guessed the Fool."

"You think those cards'll tell you the truth?" I said, handing it back.

He shrugged, tucking the deck away. "I never heard of anything or anybody that'll tell you the truth. But I'll buy your story."

"Good. What does the Hanged Man mean?"

"That you're not as smart as you think you are."

"Aw, I never thought I was as smart as I think I am. My turn for a question?"

"Sure. Why not?"

"Why would you care what I do with my nights off?"

"I don't. But if Halliday's making some bonehead play, I got to care."

"What're you, his babysitter?"

"Yes, friend," he said grimly. "That is exactly what I am."

"Why would he take that, from a rival organization?"

He made a sharp sound between his teeth. "He thinks he's got an organization. He thinks he's a rival. Lance Bejesus Halliday For my sins. Some bottle-blonde rube from Porter, Michigan."

"Porter, huh? You've been doing some studying."

He shook his head. "A guy like Halliday, you wind up knowing all kinds of things about him you wish to God you didn't know."

"I don't think the hair's a dye job."

"Great. Now that's another thing I know."

"Why does Burri put you to the trouble?"

"Grandpa Burri," he told the ceiling, eyes closed, "is a nice old grandpa who loves children. He wants them to learn. Me, I'm a bachelor."

"Why don't you give me a job? I could use one."

"Friend, a Mau-Mau like you is the last thing I need. But after last night, I'll tell you. You ever wanna pick up the gloves again, let me know. You ain't too old."

"How do you know I used to fight?"

"I told you," he said. "This town's full of little punks you wind up knowing things about. This is your stop."

I peered out through the black window. We were back in front of the Harmon Court. I got out and said, "Well, don't be strangers. Now that you know the way."

I shuffled off, leaving the door open. It was childish, but I was tired of being hey-you'ed by hoods.

The phone was ringing as I came up the walk. It stopped as I was opening the door. The clock said 9:25. I always sleep later than I think I do. I picked up the phone, called Mattie Reece, and said, "Listen. I need a favor from your cop friends. Halliday's from Porter, Michigan. I don't know what name he had back then, but a guy late twenties, his looks, tailback on the high school team, you think you could see what they've got? Can't be that big a place. Why don't you talk to Mc Donald? He knows a few things, and doesn't mind telling what he knows."

"Why would I bother?" Mattie said.

"I'll tell you how it was with Rebecca."

"Jesus, don't. I got to go home to my wife," he said, and hung up.

I sat there a while, thinking about the Hanged Man. Then I got out a sheet of paper and wrote down Scarpa's license plate number, before I forgot.

The phone started ringing again as I got into bed.

I let it.

9

Business Card

It rang an hour later while I was shaving, and I ignored that, too. When it came to breakfast, I found there wasn't a damn thing left in the house. There were five pieces of bread, some old meatloaf, and ketchup. I had two meatloaf sandwiches and a piece of bread, and that was that. I called Joanie Healey at the courthouse and gave her the number of Halliday's Lincoln. I looked over my suit. It wasn't bad, and I put it back on. Then I took it off and put on just the jacket over a yellow polo shirt, my shoulder holster, and slacks. A sports jacket would have been better, but I don't have one. I got out my .44, cleaned and loaded it, and adjusted the holster until it sat right. I put on sunglasses. They weren't the right kind, but I looked like just enough of a damn fool, and I tucked a steno pad in my pocket and drove over to the Gellar Agency.

Alban Gellar had made his bones as a cameraman at UFA and gone on to work with Pabst. I'd seen some of his old stuff. He had a pretty good eye. He was one of these painterly guys. He'd gotten out of Berlin while the getting was good and then had to think fast when he hit L.A.. One thing, he was flexible. Gellar was Viennese, originally, and in Vienna everyone's supposed to be about half an artist. In L.A., everyone's supposed to be rich. He didn't know any rich cinematographers. What, he must've asked himself, would I be if I wasn't a cameraman? A pimp, probably, but he didn't know any rich pimps, either. Still, he'd always helped get little parts for little honeys, and now he started to work at it, and take a commission. Twenty years on, Ollie Gellar had a tidy little office on DeLongpre and a fourteen-room house in Beverly Glen. He had no stars in his stable, and no serious actor would go near him, but the TV and B movie folks called him first to get someone who wasn't too expensive or too good. He was as honest as anybody else, and better organized than most, the way you have to be when you're selling cut-price goods in bulk. Every has-been, thick-tongued beauty queen, and non-actor in town was in his files. I was in there myself, assuming he hadn't gotten around to throwing me out.

Lately Gellar had left the actual work to a series of little honeys, each one cute as a button and sharp as a knife. When I came in, the current incumbent was sitting at the reception desk, behind a plaque reading L. R. BELLINGER. She was fox-faced, with curly russet hair. She didn't have much upstairs or down, but she did have self-confidence, and I guess she deserved to. She had one other thing, something you don't get much out here, and that's an accent. It was pure Georgia honeysuckle, and most girls would've gotten rid of it in case Darryl Zanuck might not like it.

She wasn't stingy with it, either, and there was a whole waiting room full of hopeful actors who got their share. They all wanted to see Ollie, and they all got told he was in conference. Some had appointments with him. He was still in conference. Most of them handed over a small sheaf of glossies, answered half a dozen quick questions, and were back on the street before they could get their charm out of first gear. One matronly woman got a dozen questions and a minute of finger-drumming, then was told to call back that afternoon. One courtly old gent with silvery temples got dead silence and a stare. He put his head shots away and left without arguing. Near noon there was a lull, and I got up and went over to the desk.

"Well," she said brightly, "aren't you the politest old boy."

"I've been called a lot of things. But I think that's a new one."

"You let *all* these nice people ahead of you. Even the ones who came in after! Now, you sure you weren't just trying to get me alone so's you could make a pass?"

"I wish I were that bright."

"Well, as it happens, cuz, you're in luck. Because I believe I might have something right here for you this very afternoon. Ever done a wrestling picture?"

"Yes."

"It's not a speaking part, you know."

"It wouldn't be. Look, Miss Bellinger, I'm not an actor, or not any more. My name's Ray Corson. I'm doing some preliminary casting for Republic."

"Is that a fact. And you came *all* the way over here your own self? Now I call that nice. Got a business card?"

I shook my head. "I'm not on the payroll, really. I just sort of do odd jobs. A little writing, a little reading. Piecework. Morris Severin asked me to flesh out a treat-

ment for him. He thinks it'd settle his thinking if he could
see it cast. It's a Musketeer kind of thing, sword-fighting,
swinging from ropes, the bit, and we need a young guy
who moves well, a fair, handsome guy. And I have to tell
you, we need him cheap." She inclined her head under-
standingly. I shook mine. "I mean cheap even for
Republic. I'll be frank. If this one can't be made for a
nickel, it won't be made. And I'd sort of like to see it
made. It would be— Well, I might get a business card out
of it. We're looking for guys other people might've taken
a pass on, and someone mentioned a TV actor called
Larry Halliday."

"Lance Halliday."

"That's it."

"And you're working for Severin."

"Shouldn't I be?"

"What if I called him up?"

I nodded. "That's a good idea. It's so easy to get
through to him, and he just loves phone calls." I glared at
her from under my eyebrows and croaked, *"Explain to
me again, young lady, why somebody gave you your job."*

She laughed. "I guess you do know Morrie. I don't
know why I'm not trusting you. Mostly they have us send
the shots over. We don't get many walk-ins."

"Well, I'm new at this. Probably I'm doing it all wrong.
Maybe you could give me a little coaching."

"Easy, cuz," she said. "Stick to the menu, and don't
order what you can't afford." She got up, smoothed down
her dress—it was already smooth—and turned to open
the inner door. I followed her into Gellar's office. It was
empty. "Mr. Gellar is in conference," she said. "Deep,
deep in conference."

One wall of the room was file cabinets from floor to
ceiling. She fetched out a file, perched on the corner of
Gellar's desk, and crossed her legs. They were worth

crossing. "What does the L. R. stand for?" I asked.

"Why don't we stick with Miss Bellinger for now? All righty. Mr. Halliday is not what you'd call an active file. He hasn't done any adventure, really. He hasn't really done much of anything. Except screen tests. Mr. Halliday has tested for every studio in town. He was a swim coach in *Million Dollar Mermaid*. I guess you could say that was his career high. He stood around in a swimming suit, which he does *very* well, and said 'Hello Annette' to Esther Williams. I wish I could say we got him that one. We did get him a toothpaste commercial. That old boy has teeth you simply would not credit."

"I suppose teeth won't hurt us. Can he fence, dance, anything like that?"

"Mr. Corson, do you really not know what Lance Halliday does these days?"

"No. What?"

"He's, ah. He's moved over into production. Sort of like yourself, Mr. Corson."

"He can't be making much of a success of it, or I'd have heard. Anyway, maybe he'd like another crack at the limelight. If you don't represent him now, how would I go about getting in touch?"

"Mr. Corson. What do you really want?"

"It would be my life's dream if you cared what I really want."

"And here you promised me you wouldn't make a pass."

"No, I just promised you I wasn't that bright."

"I've figured it out," said Miss Bellinger. "You're a detective on the case. One of these super-sleuths. You're hot on the trail. Well, Mr. Corson, I'm going to teach you a little trick you can show all your gumshoe friends," She pulled a phone book from the shelf, flipped through it, and turned it to face me. She tapped the page with a slim forefinger. I saw a listing for Halliday Productions, with an address on Cahuenga, out on the other side of the hills.

"Thanks," I said, getting out my steno pad.

"Show you another trick," she said. She flipped through the book and turned it to me again. This time she pointed to a listing for L. R. Bellinger.

I wrote down the number and address. "What does the L. R. stand for?" I said.

"Lisa Rae," she said.

"Pretty name," I said.

10
Office

Halliday's office was in one of those modernistic buildings that look old six months after they're built. It had a two-story lobby with a streaked glass wall in front and a steel and terrazzo staircase in back. Everything was covered in dusty green bathroom tile. It was trying hard not to seem cheap. It looked like Rebecca's boarding house in a ten-dollar suit. As I climbed the stairs, I was getting my story straight. I'd be an out-of-work actor too stupid to know what Halliday Productions did. If Halliday was there, I'd come round to say we'd got off on the wrong foot last night. As it happened, nobody was there. I knocked, rattled the knob, and went down the back stairs, pulling some surgical gloves from my pocket. I had a carton of them from an OR nurse I knew with more freckles more places than you'd think was possible.

I got the gloves on, came back up quietly, and took a strip of celluloid from my wallet. It was a four-inch length of 35-millimeter film snipped from a Republic quickie called *Aloha Samoa*. It used to show a sleepy lagoon jeweled with sunlight, but I'd worn most of the emulsion off. I had three of these strips. A single thickness was too limp for the lock, but two did the trick, and I leaned my shoulder into the door and cuddled it open almost silently. I locked it behind me and looked around. It was a single room with a single desk. I didn't like it. I walked to the window and opened it. A ten-foot drop to the asphalt parking lot in front, in full view of the road. I liked it less. I drew a finger across the seat of the chair, hoping for a film of dust. There wasn't much. That chair was getting sat in, though not every day. I decided, the hell, if Halliday showed, I'd shoot him and collect my money.

In the kneehole drawer I found two big checkbooks, the sort with three checks per page. One book was for Halliday Productions, the other for something called Prestige Enterprises. According to the stubs, the Halliday checkbook wasn't used for much but paying the office rent and phone. The Prestige book was working harder: film stock, processing and duplicating, some equipment rentals, editing-room time, lights, and the occasional projector. Both showed regular cash deposits and irregular cash withdrawals, probably to pay the talent. I suppose that sort of thing's a cash business. I was aware of the tiny noises any building makes, of the swish of cars passing on Cahuenga, of the big window at my back. I kept having the idea that if I turned around, I'd see someone outside the window making faces at me. But the nice thing about nerves is, all you have to do is ignore them. There was an address book on the desk by the phone, which seemed to be full of the same suppliers from the checkbook. In the back were a few pages with first names and phone numbers, no last names or addresses, in no special order, and most of the names crossed out. That would be the talent, and I copied down ten at random, half of them crossed-out, half current. There was nothing else in the top drawer except a roll of stamps in the pencil trough. I was out of stamps and I took a few.

In the top right-hand drawer were two boxes of letterhead, one for Halliday, one for Prestige. The addresses were the same. I took a half-dozen sheets of each, folded them carefully, and tucked them in my pocket with some matching envelopes. There was a little packet of business cards held together with a rubber band. The cards bore no name or phone number, just an address out in the valley somewhere. I heard footsteps coming up the front stairs, put the cards down, and got out my gun. The footsteps came closer and then got fainter, and I heard a key going into a lock down the hall. I waited until I heard the door shut. I put my gun away, slipped out one of the cards, and tucked it in my wallet.

I opened the bottom right-hand drawer and found a carton of flashbulbs and a carton of .38 bullets. I closed it. There weren't any left-hand drawers, so I went over the filing cabinets. The first was all receipted bills to Prestige. I went back, got out the Prestige checkbook, and compared a few bills with the check stubs. The amounts matched up. I put the checkbook away. The next three cabinets you could have entertained yourself with a while. They contained packaged sets of photographs of the sort that are called either Artistic or Specialized. The Artistic ones were all bathing beauties who'd forgotten their suits. None of them appeared to have noticed it yet, and you'd have felt like a heel for telling them. They wore big smiles that seemed to say *Isn't this fun?* except for a few who were on the phone and seemed to say *Be with you in a minute*. The Specialized ones were all of people I didn't know, doing things to each other that I was roughly familiar with. The Specialized people all seemed to be very tan or very pale. They had a stunned look, like trophies on a rec room wall.

The last cabinet was locked, and I got out my picks and muttered bad words at myself for ten minutes. I left scratches, too, for anybody looking close. I stink at that stuff. Inside was nothing but two books. One of them seemed like a list of steady customers, with addresses and phones. None of them would know anything useful and I put it away. The other was a scrapbook. There were a few different head shots of Halliday, and then a production still from a picture called *Dusk on the Danube*, showing a ballroom full of dancing couples. I finally picked out Halliday in a hussar's uniform, standing by a column. The next page showed Halliday saying hello to Esther Williams, and there was another still of just him in his old-time bathing suit, down on one knee holding a whistle on a lanyard around his neck, and smiling into the distance. There were a dozen pages of publicity stuff from *Million Dollar Mermaid*, none of it mentioning him. Then a toothpaste ad, with Halliday smiling and holding a brush. The rest of the book was empty. I put it back, locked the cabinet again, shut the window, locked the office door behind me, and went down the back stairs, pulling off my gloves.

It was getting dusk but I wasn't sure I felt like dinner yet. I had that sickish, sort of metallic feeling inside, like nothing I ate would taste very good.

What had I scraped up so far? A handsome little hood named Halliday who peddled smut because they wouldn't let him be a movie star. What did he want? To be a bigger hood. To burn girls' faces who turned him down. To say hi to Esther Williams again.

Then there was a bigger hood named Scarpa who'd

been told off to keep an eye on Halliday. What did he want? To not be bothered with little punks like Halliday and me.

Then there was a great big hood named Burri who'd done the telling. What did he want? A nice civilized drink and some little dry cookies. He was an old man, and wanted everything nice. What would he do to someone who kept things from being nice?

Halliday was too ambitious for Burri, too podunk for Scarpa, too bughouse for Rebecca. It was nice to know he was everybody's problem, not just mine. There ought to be a way to make that work for me. It was right there staring at me, if I had any brains.

That was a big if.

I took La Brea down to 10, headed west, turned off on National, and cruised through Palms. There were some nice little houses there, but nothing I'd picture a crime boss in. Halliday's was at 3235 Shippie Avenue. It was a small two-story mock-Tudor with a half-timbered front, and the lawn was kept nice. The driveway was full of cars, and there were cars parked solid all up and down the block. There was someone standing in the driveway watching the cars go by. He watched me drive up, and he watched me keep driving on past. I wondered again what Halliday wanted with so many guys. I took the next left and thought about circling the block. Maybe I could park somewhere and find a way to work in close to the house. Maybe there was some way to hear what was going on inside. Maybe I could creep down the chimney like Old Saint Nick. The cars hadn't looked nice enough to be capos' cars. There hadn't been enough light and noise for a party. It might have been Halliday rounding up his people for some kind of staff meeting. What kind? I drove around for a while, thinking thoughts. But only one of them turned out to be useful: I thought if I went down to Annie Jay's and ordered a bloody ribeye, mashed potatoes, and apple pie with cheddar, it would be pretty good. And it was.

11
Pool

The pool at the motel is pretty nasty-looking and not many people use it. I've never been in myself except when I'm cleaning it, and I don't clean it often. The next morning, though, I woke up to the sound of splashing. I peeked through the curtains and saw a little heap of clothes on the concrete and a woman in the water, swimming laps smoothly and very rapidly.

I couldn't see her face, but she wasn't wearing a cap and the hair streaming down her back was dark gold. Her arms and legs went on a long way. I put some pants and a shirt on and came outside. She didn't seem to need to breathe. It took her two strokes to cross the pool the long way, and I had the idea she was shortening her stroke so she could fit two of them in. Each time she reached the end, she rolled smoothly under like a seal and reappeared moving fast in the opposite direction. I thought of how birds are awkward when they walk, but graceful in their own natural element. I thought a lot of the crap you think when you're falling. I went inside and found a clean towel. When I came out again, Rebecca was climbing out of the pool, wearing a blue one-piece racing suit. Her hair hung in dark gold ropes down her face and neck. I handed her the towel and she dried her face and arms. She looked healthy and carefree and about fourteen. "I came snooping by the other day and saw you had a pool," she said. "We don't have one at home. I wish we did."

"It's pretty nasty in there."

"Oh, that stuff doesn't hurt you. That's just algae. Didn't you ever swim in a pond? Isn't someone supposed to be skimming it, though?"

"They don't pay me enough."

"That's the one thing I could always really do, swim. In high school I was northeastern champion three years running in hundred crawl and fifteen hundred back. I think if there was such a thing as professional swimmers, I wouldn't've bothered with the actress stuff. But you can't make money swimming."

She looked blissfully happy. She bent quickly to towel her legs, then raised her arms and worked the towel roughly through her hair, smiling with closed eyes into the sun. She opened her eyes again and her smile turned mocking. I'd been staring at her endowments, and she'd noticed it first. I don't look like the kind that blushes, and I'm not, but I felt my face redden and prickle. "Sorry," I said. "They really are the eighth and ninth wonders, aren't they? Jesus, imagine being you and having them around all the time."

"You can touch one for a dollar," she said.

"What?"

"Give me a dollar," she said, drying her back.

After a moment, I took a dollar from my pocket and handed it to her. She folded it twice and tucked it under the right strap of her suit, then swung my towel around her shoulders like a shawl. Beneath it, she lowered her left strap. She took hold of my right hand, slipped it under the towel, and placed it on her breast. It was heavy and firm. The skin was still cold and goose-pimpled, but I could feel the heat inside.

She said, "Where the hell have you been for the last two days?"

I blinked and would have jerked my hand back, but she had a good grip on my wrist. Her eyes were pale and hard.

"Where the hell have you been?" she said.

"Working," I said.

"Working how? For whom? I've been trying to call you for two goddamned days."

"I was out."

"Where?"

"First night? The Centaur. I wanted to see Halliday."

"My God. You didn't talk to him, did you?"

"Yeah, we had a nice chat. Rebecca—"

"Oh my God. My God. I'm surprised he didn't set the dogs on you."

"He did."

"I wish they tore your head off. My God, what a bungler. Do you want to spoil everything? Do you want to get my face burnt off?"

I was having a hard time paying attention. I was pretty wrought up and afraid someone would look out a window and see. Rebecca was crisp and composed. The breast in my palm seemed to crowd out all my thoughts. I gave it a little squeeze. That seemed to be included in the rental. I said, "No."

"And all day yesterday?"

"I did a little research. I checked out Halliday's office."

"Checked out?"

"I broke in and had a look around."

"You broke in. In the middle of the day? And when he finds somebody's broken into his office?"

"There's no reason for him to need to know." I couldn't even talk properly. "Rebecca, I'm looking for a lever. There seems to be some rivalry with the Scarpa—"

"*That's* what you found out? Everyone knows that."

"I didn't, and you didn't tell me. Becky, Halliday's low man on the totem pole and trying to wriggle up. If he's, ah, Jesus." I took a breath. "If he's been wriggling onto Scarpa's turf, maybe we can use the threat of Scarpa to control him."

"This is all pretty iffy."

I nodded and reached for the other breast with my free hand. She pushed it away. "I said you could touch *one*."

I dug in my pocket left-handed and held out another dollar.

"The second one," she said seriously, "is twenty dollars."

I stared, then said, "The hell with it. It's probably just like the first one."

She stepped back and tucked herself away.

"I've been hiding in my room for two days," she said, "not knowing what in God's name was going on, my heart in my mouth every time I had to open my door and walk down to the phone, while you ran around town playing Private Eye and Daring Daylight Burglar." She turned away from me and pulled on her slacks. Dark marks like peonies bloomed on the seat. She slipped into a white blouse and knotted it savagely at the waist. "I never was too good at picking 'em, and I guess I'm still not. But what I do know how to do is cut my losses. You've got twenty-four hours, Ray. Twenty-four hours to do something. To bring me something better than some theory— a plan, a solid plan—or admit you're just another false alarm."

She yanked on her sandals and stalked away from me without a backward look.

I stood there, rubbing my right palm with my left thumb.

12
Suit

I arrived at the Centaur that night a bit before nine, because I'd arrived there just before nine on Tuesday and found Burri in his banquette. He was there again. Scarpa was with him. Burri's bodyguards were at the bar. They watched me walk up with no special interest, but they watched. I didn't see Green Eyes or Round Head anywhere. Then Scarpa saw me, and then Burri did, and opened his hands in a big look-who's-here gesture, and I walked over to the table. Burri raised a bony finger and a waitress trotted over in another little gold dress. She was a chubby little sweetie with coppery hair. She needed a lot more cloth of gold than the gazelle did to keep her decent. She wasn't getting it. Burri pointed at me and said, "This young man requires a gimlet. A gimlet, do I seem to recall that this is your drink?"

I never wanted to see another goddamned stinking gimlet as long as I lived.

I sat down, saying, "Thanks."

"Now," Burri said. "*This* is nice. You came to keep an old man company."

"No, sir," I said.

"No?"

"No. I'm taking your advice, Mr. Burri, and passing up that other opportunity we were discussing. You mentioned the possibility of a job. I came to see if I could get it."

"There," Burri said, smiling at Scarpa. "You see? God provides."

"Nice of Him," Scarpa said woodenly.

"I would like to introduce you to a fine young man of

my acquaintance, a Mr. Corson, but why do I have this feeling that I don't need to?"

"We've met," Scarpa said.

"Is this so?" Burri asked me. "This is what you do, go around meeting everybody?"

"I get lonesome," I said.

"Well, then everybody knows everybody," Burri said. "Very good. Now, I should admit that I have already seen enough of you, young man, to form for myself a preliminary opinion of your character. And I believe you might be suitable for a small matter Mr. Scarpa and I were discussing. Lenny, you agree?"

"*Padrone*, this is the man from the Jade Mountain. That I was telling you about."

"This?" Burri said wonderingly. "This is the guy?"

"I'm afraid so," I said.

Burri began to giggle. "You're the one? The one with Lance's people? You're in the Chink place, and they both got guns, and you got nothing, just your bare fanny, and you go in there and you put them both in the hospital?"

"It seemed like a good idea at the time."

"This tickles me," Burri said, wheezing. "This tickles me. I don't believe I'm mistaken in saying that this is quite something. What, Leonardo, you don't like it? You don't think it's funny?"

"You can have my share," Scarpa said.

"Ah, Leonardo, it's a terrible thing, to be such a young man and already so serious. You mustn't lose your sense of humor, Leonardo. Because really, we're all just a little joke God is having. Ah? The nuns didn't teach you that? You didn't ask them the right questions."

Burri grinned at me, and for just a moment, I saw Scarpa examining him. It was a calm look, a look I'd seen before. Like a butcher with his cleaver raised, measuring by eye.

By the time Burri turned back to Scarpa, still grinning, the look was gone.

Burri said, "Now, you two are both fine, able young men, and I'm sure you can work together constructively."

"I can work with anybody," Scarpa said.

"That's fine now," Burri said.

I said, "If—"

"I think that we're all in agreement now," Burri said.

I said, "Thanks, Mr. Burri."

Scarpa stood and said, "Come into the office."

"But he hasn't gotten his drink!" Burri said.

"I'll *get* him a drink," Scarpa said. "Let's go."

I followed him across the big room and through a door at the end of the bar. As it swung shut behind me, the music and the roar of the big nightclub fell away to a whisper. Soundproofed. To our right was a narrow staircase, windowless and two stories tall, covered with spotless ivory carpeting, and Scarpa motioned me ahead. I started climbing the stairs ahead of him. At the top was another door, one with no knob. "Push it," Scarpa said behind me. I pressed on the door. After a moment, there was a click and it swung inwards, and we stepped into a good-sized office, carpeted in taupe, with milk-glass sconces along the walls. The door swung silently shut behind us and the faint noise of the club abruptly ceased. It was quiet enough that I could hear the hum of the electric clock. Before me was a big desk of bird's-eye maple and black glass, and beside it, a row of tall windows looking out over a dark, wooded slope. Three comfortable armchairs faced the desk, each with a small glass table beside it. A sofa took up the wall across from the windows. I looked behind me and saw a counter with a row of circular grilles along it, a small red stud and a black number next to each. On the wall above it was a numbered floor plan of the club. I strolled over to the window and looked down at a sunken loading dock. It was about fifty feet down to the cement. Scarpa seated himself behind the desk and sighed.

"I guess I was born to be a babysitter," he said.

There was another grille set into his desk, and he leaned toward it, pressed a stud, and said, "Two gins." He leaned back. "I hate gimlets. I hate goddamn lime juice. You like gimlets?"

"Not anymore. I was drinking them that night at the Jade Mountain."

He let out a little huff of laughter. "You don't know what the hell you're doing, do you?"

I shrugged, looking out the window. "I'll find out."

"Getting ready to jump?"

"Not till I've had my drink."

"What would you've done if you came in here and met Halliday instead?"

"Smiled pretty," I dropped into one of the armchairs.

"You know," Scarpa said. "The old man likes to talk like a fool. He enjoys it. But if he was really such an old fool, somebody would have taken care of him by now."

The door behind Scarpa's desk opened and the gazelle stepped through it, carrying a tray with two tall gins. Through the door as she closed it, I glimpsed what looked like an apartment decorated in ivory and taupe. She set a drink on a coaster at Scarpa's elbow, then came around the desk, and I saw that she wore no shoes or stockings, just the little gold dress. She set the other drink on the table by my chair, then laid the empty tray on the corner of Scarpa's desk, walked around behind his chair, and ran her fingers down his temples. She took hold of his shoulders and began to knead them. Neither had stopped looking at me.

"I dunno," Scarpa said. "What does he look like to you? To me, he just looks like a mutt."

"Mutts come all kinds," she remarked, digging her thumbs in.

I sipped my drink. Scarpa ignored his. She stopped rubbing his shoulders and draped her arms loosely around him, resting her belly against his nape. He pushed her away with an irritable shove of his head, and she seated herself on the credenza behind him and rested her bare feet on the desktop, knees together. Scarpa rose and came out from behind the desk.

"Stand up," he said.

I stood up.

"Come over where I can see you."

I stepped forward. He took hold of my lapel and rubbed it between his fingers. "You like this suit?"

"Why would I?" I said.

He opened my jacket, lifted out my gun, and let it slip back into its holster, nodding. "You don't work with jeweler's tools."

He strolled around behind me and I felt him try to brush something off my shoulder. He ambled back into view. He lifted my tie and examined it. It was a plain deep yellow silk tie.

"The tie's all right," he decided.

He let it fall and slammed his fist into my stomach.

Scarpa could hit, and he gave me plenty. But he'd also given me all week to get set. I rocked back on my heels and then looked at the gazelle to take my mind off it. Her mouth was open, and I held mine shut and smiled at her. You've got to take the first breath right away, and then the next ones are easier. Scarpa was standing before me, hands on hips, staring up at me, chin out, waiting.

"Feel better now?" I said. My voice was tight.

"I do," he said. "I guess you can screw the lid on it after all."

He leaned back against the edge of his desk, hands in his pockets.

He said, "I make you as some kind of hick, right? But you got a head. You got eyes. You got a mouth, too, but all right. All right. Sometimes the old man still sees things first."

Now she saw I was okay, the gazelle decided she'd liked me being hit just fine. There was never a dull moment with me around. She was showing me just about all the legs she had. It was more legs than I thought one girl was allowed.

Scarpa said, "Scamper, honey."

She picked up the tray and went back through the door behind the desk. It closed the way it had opened, without a sound.

"Here's the thing," Scarpa told me. "We sell a lot to movie people. But the last couple three months, I've lost a number of my nice steady customers. I don't have any competition I know of, not in that part of town. There's four five guys, and some of them have guys, and they compete with each other, but they all get their stuff from me. I've talked to my neighbors. I think they're on the level. So it's a new guy, an independent. Maybe he's a movie guy himself. I wanna talk to him."

I said, "I'm not a finger man, Lenny. If you use me that way, you'll find I'm more trouble than I'm worth."

"Just talk, to begin with. I don't waste that stuff."

"Uh huh."

"If I wanted him iced," he said patiently, "would I have you bring him to me? Think I still do that kind of work myself?"

"Okay. I don't."

"You work for me now. So I don't need as much mouth from you as I been getting."

"All right. I'll want some money."

"You'll get paid when you show you're worth paying."

"I'll have to be nice to people. I'll probably have to make a buy myself."

"All right." He pulled out his wallet, counted off two fifties and five twenties, and handed them over. New bills, fresh from the bank. Two weeks' work for Nestor. He took out a small leather notebook and began writing. "You find the guy, you call this number. I don't care what time it is."

He tore out the sheet, turned it over, and began writing again. "And this, this is my tailor. You're gonna be there tomorrow morning when he opens at eight. He'll be expecting you. Don't tell him what you want. He'll give you what I want. The tie's all right. You can keep the tie. But if I gotta look at you? It's not gonna be in that suit."

13
Coast Highway

Joseph Callender, Suitings wasn't right on Rodeo Drive, but just around the corner on Brighton, behind a door that was freshly painted green but didn't look like much and up a flight of stairs with gleaming black marble treads. There wasn't any sign out front. Mr. Callender was there, sirring away at me, when I reached the top of the stairs at eight the next morning. There was no one thing about his clothes you'd notice, but he was about sixty and pear-shaped and the way he dressed, he made you wish you were sixty and pear-shaped, too. I thought I might be a problem for him but he said I was actually a fairly classic 50 Long and wouldn't need much work. I said that was good to know. He ran a tape over me just to make sure, dictating to an assistant the while, and took tracings of my stocking feet, and then sat me down in a green leather chair with a *Tribune* that was hot and flat, as if it had just been ironed, and some coffee in a cup I was kind of proud of myself for not breaking. In the next half hour three boys came up the stairs, loaded down with packages from some of the stores around the corner: Carroll & Co. and Lanzetti and D. Salzburg. Callender had me try on suits until he found one he could live with, then touched it here and there with chalk. He asked whether I'd need a little extra room under the left arm. I said I carried a .44 Python and should I have brought it? He said he'd seen them. He gave the jacket to one assistant and the pants to another, then sat me down and poured me more coffee, and I asked if he usually did alterations on off-the-rack clothes. He said that for a customer like Mr. Scarpa one made exceptions. I said yes, one did.

He had the whole shop working at once, it looked like, and got me out the door in under three hours. It was a little before noon when I pulled back into the lot at home. Rebecca was there, sitting in her convertible in a big sun hat and sunglasses. She took off the glasses when she saw me, and got out of her car, and I parked and walked over to meet her. I was wearing a sharkskin suit like Scarpa's, only a darker gray they called oxford, a white button-down shirt—I had three more in the car, wrapped in paper—a snap-brim hat with a midnight blue band, black wingtips that shone dully, like obsidian, gray silk socks—I had a dozen of those—and my tie. I stood before her and held out my arms. "This is it," I said. "As

Sinatra as I'll ever get."

She shook her head helplessly. "All right," she said. "Tell me."

"Last night Lenny Scarpa made me one of his gentlemen-in-waiting. He didn't like my clothes, so he sent me to his tailor this morning. They let me keep my tie."

"You got a job with Scarpa," she said.

"Someone's been poaching his snowbirds. He hired me to find out who. If it's Halliday, we'll have a number of angles to play, plus Scarpa's backing. If it's not, we've still got more leverage then we did. I know you wanted a plan, and this is a little vaguer than that, but it's what I've got. If it doesn't sound good, you can have your money back."

"You're working for Scarpa," she said again, like somebody had sapped her and she was waiting to fall down.

Then, starting with the eyes, a smile spread over her face. You've never seen a smile like that.

I pity you.

She said, "You're— You really are the most amazing man I have ever met in my life."

"You ought to get out more."

"That is brilliant. That is better than anything I could possibly— It's *perfect*. I've been sitting here, waiting to tell you that I'd been, um, unreasonable is a kind word, and that you could have more time, if you needed it, and all the while you were—" She shook her head. "I thought you'd run off again. I thought you'd run off. Not that I'd have blamed you. I was horrible to you yesterday, and I've also been waiting here to apologize."

"That's all right. It wasn't all bad."

"I suppose," she said, flushing a little. "Anyhow, Ray, I'm sorry. I act badly when I'm frightened. I've spent too much time sitting in my room being frightened."

"Maybe we can fix that."

"I think you can. I know you can. This morning I know you can do anything."

"Thanks."

"Isn't it a beautiful morning?"

"It's almost a beautiful afternoon."

"Come on," she said. "Let's go for a ride."

I got in the car, and she pulled out and headed down Hawthorne to Rosecranz, then swung north on Vista del Mar, and we went cruising up the coast with the big silver tanks of the refinery on one side and the waves along the other. People say the weather's always perfect in L.A., but what they really mean is always sunny. Most of the days aren't actually perfect. That one was. Even the oil tanks looked pretty, and then we'd left them behind, and off to our right the waves were loping along, the edges like fine silver chains, seeming to braid and unbraid themselves. I come from way inland, and that stuff always stops me.

"It's worth it," she said. "Oh, it's worth the risk. I should have done this days ago."

I said, "You're not telling me that's all this heap'll do."

"No. I guess I'm not."

"C'mon, then," I said.

She eased her foot down on the gas, and the big car surged smoothly forward until the needle read 85. It wasn't anything for that car. She held it there for a minute, then said, "That's as far as I go, for now," and eased it back down to 60.

"This is some car. What are you laughing at?" I said.

She said, "You. You just sitting there with your face in the wind like, I don't know. Some big dog. I don't mean that in any bad way. It's just, you're always trying to be so tough, and here you are just riding along in the sun and enjoying it so much."

"It's a nice day."

"Isn't it?"

"It's not a bad car, either."

"I'd like you to have something." She picked her purse up from the floor under her knees, set it on her lap, and started rummaging in it one-handed.

"Don't run us off the road," I said.

She held out a dollar bill, folded twice. "Here."

"What's this?"

"It's from yesterday. I wish you'd take it back."

"What for? You—"

"No, please. Please don't say whatever you were about to say about, I don't know. Services rendered or goods delivered or whatever hard-boiled wisecrack it was. I wish you'd please just take it. Because I think I was very ugly to you, and if I at least didn't make you give me a dollar, then, well, I don't know, then whatever it was was something else. Nicer. Not just me trying to make a monkey of you."

"What would it've been? Without the dollar?" I said, taking the money. "Thanks."

"I don't know. Something just silly and, I don't know, sort of high-schoolish. I was still a nice girl in high school. Not the kind of nice girl who's never done anything, but I hadn't done everything, and I was still nice to people. I had a beau and I was true to him."

"Yeah? Was he nice too?"

"Very nice. He was my own true love."

"You had one of those?"

"Yes. Just one."

"They say that's all you need."

"They say."

"What was nice about him?"

"He was inquisitive."

"I guess that's good. What happened?"

"Well, after a few years, I guess he sort of stopped being nice. He was a nice boy, but he didn't turn out to be a nice man."

"What did you do?"

"I guess I stopped being nice, too. He was my own true love, and I wanted to keep him company."

"Then what?"

"Then it was over. My God, to think about me being still nice. How long has it been since you were a nice boy?"

"I don't know that I was ever particularly nice."

"Please don't say that," she said. "It can't be true. You're nice now, in some ways."

"I think I'm about as nice now as I ever was. I used to be dumber."

"I can't imagine you being dumb. But I can imagine you being nice in an angry, rough way, and sort of serious. Maybe too serious. Were you always a big reader?"

"I never finished high school."

"I know that. Mattie told me. That's not what I'm talking about, that's just you being hard-boiled again. Were you a reader?"

"I always liked books pretty well."

"Why didn't you finish high school?"

"I went out on the road. How'd you know that about the books? Mattie?"

"No, I guessed it about you. You look at everything as if it was a problem you had to study up on."

"I do, huh."

"Yes. You have this patient look, like you're listening very carefully to find out how we've all screwed everything up, so you can fix it."

"Sounds charming."

"Were you the one in the family that always thought it

was his job to fix everything? And then, when everything started going to hell, you tried to stop it and couldn't?"

After a moment I said, "You're a good guesser. What makes you say things went to hell?"

"Because you went on the road before you finished high school. You wouldn't have, not so young, if you could still have stood it there. If there was anyone left there who could care for you."

"I guess we all did what we needed to."

"You must've had to leave all your books behind," she said softly.

We were silent.

"*Well,*" she said very brightly. "*I* never opened a book I didn't have to. Or had an idea in my head I didn't have to. I read lots of movie magazines and if you'd known me then you'd have thought I was one Dumb Dora. You would have sneered at my movie magazines."

"You know," I said, "you're right. I would've."

"You never read any yourself?"

"All I could get my hands on," I said, and she laughed. I laughed, too.

"But you would've tried to stop me reading them," she said. "You would have tried to improve my mind."

"I wouldn't have had the nerve to talk to you."

"Maybe I would have talked to you. Do you think we'd have liked each other? Back when we were nice kids, reading movie magazines? I know you're a little older, but let's say."

"I didn't like nice girls."

"Hard-boiled," she said warningly.

"No, it's true. I liked Sin. I was praying for a girl who'd, you know, pull the book out of my hands and the glasses off my face, even though I didn't wear glasses, and, you know, corrupt me. I thought I was a very serious guy, too, but I was hoping some red-hot mama would come along and make a wolf of me."

"And what happened?"

"That's what happened."

"Oh ho."

"Took a few years, though."

"So I'd've been too nice to be your girl. But maybe we could have been friends?"

"If you'd ever talked to me, I'd have fainted."

"And after I threw a bucket of water over you and woke you up?"

"Then I'd have made fun of your movie magazines."

"And after I kicked you in the shins?"

"Then I guess we might have been friends. I don't know, Rebecca. To tell the truth, you play-act so much, I couldn't say what you'd be like if you stopped."

"Neither could I," she said sadly. "I'm play-acting now?"

"I couldn't tell you, Rebecca."

"Neither could I," she said again.

We'd jogged through town just past the airport and were back on the Coast Highway now, and the road was rising as we came around the curve toward Malibu. I could see Point Dume off in the distance.

I said, "Aw, hell, Rebecca. I'm sorry. The truth is, I may be too old to faint, but you pretty much scare me now."

"I scare all the boys," she said. "All of them with any brains. Well, so much for our beautiful friendship."

"Even if it never happened," I said, "it was nice while it lasted."

"Yes, at least we've got our memories."

"Yeah."

"Our movie magazines. Your glasses."

"Your bucket."

"Do you know what I really would've said to you, Ray?

If I were your friend?"

"What?"

"I'd tell you, stay away from that Rebecca girl." She leaned toward me. "I'd tell you: *Run, run as fast as you can!*" She fell back against the seat, laughing.

"Yeah," I said. "But if I was your friend, I'd say, Sorry, I'm sticking around anyway."

"So I guess it wouldn't matter, me warning you."

"I guess not."

"You keep looking back in the mirror. Why do you keep looking in the mirror?"

"Rebecca?"

"Yes? What's back there?"

"You wouldn't set me up, now, would you?"

"What do you mean?" she said.

"The same car's been behind us for the last fifteen minutes. I'm pretty sure it's been with us since we left my place."

"*It's him,*" she said in a horrible little voice with no breath, and stamped on the gas.

The big engine took hold, and I felt us both being mashed back into our seats.

14

Iron

The speedometer said 70, then 80, then 90. The wind rushed by my ears with a scraping sound.

"All right," I said. "That's enough. That's not necessary."

"He's going to burn me," she whispered. No, it was worse than whispering. "He'll burn me."

105, and starting to rock a little. Rebecca's face was

stretched taut and her lips were white, and behind the sunglasses her eyes were huge and lopsided. The cords were out on her throat. She looked as if she were forty years old and hadn't been living right. I set my hand on the back of her neck and stroked it. "It's okay, Rebecca," I said. "This isn't necessary. Just stop it."

"He's going to—"

"No. You think you're panicking," I said. "And that you can't stop. But you can, any time. You can stop now. Right now. Now just slow down."

She didn't answer.

I scooted closer, slid my left leg under both of hers and lifted my knee. The back of her knees felt delicious against my leg. I can't help it, it did. I humped up my leg under hers, and both her feet came off the pedals and the car began to slow. She stared hopelessly straight ahead, gripping the wheel, feet dangling, tears trickling down her cheeks. "That's right," I said. "That's right. You're getting it back under control now. All righty."

"I'm sorry," she said.

"You're okay now. I'm going to take my leg away. Will you hold it at 60?"

"Yes."

"Say it so I believe it."

"Yes."

I pulled my leg back and she set her foot gently on the gas. We settled in at 60.

"All right," I said. "There's someone behind us. We don't know who. If it's Halliday, he can't do anything while we're all driving along, and it won't help to put us in the ditch." I looked back again. It was still there, a big car, dark blue and gleaming in the sun. "If it's him, the one thing we don't want is to lead him to your house. So we're going to turn off in a minute, and see if whoever it is turns off with us. If he does, I'm going to meet him.

What's in the trunk?"

"What? Nothing. A spare."

"Good," I said. We'd just passed Topanga. "Take the next turnoff," I said, and started working the trunk key off the ring hanging from the steering column.

"What are you going to do?"

"If it's Halliday? Take back the initiative. Here's the turnoff."

We turned up Tuna Canyon, a dirt road crawling up a little gully full of scrub and weeds, olive and brown. If the blue car turned in, we'd know.

I said, "This's as good a place as any. Pull up over there. Now, nothing much'll probably happen, but if you see or hear anything you don't like, just take off. But don't go to your house. There's a diner called Charlie's Gold Medal on Western and 137th. Go there and tell Rina you're my friend and need to wait in the office upstairs. I'll call you there as soon as I can. If you haven't heard from me within, say, four hours, you'll have to use your judgment. All right?"

"Western and 137th," she said. "Okay. I'm sorry about before."

"Good girl," I said. "Right over here."

I was out the door while the car was still rolling and trotted around to the trunk. It was the cleanest damn trunk you ever saw. The tire iron was right where it was supposed to be. It was just the right length and weight, too, and I took a few practice cuts with it, getting used to the gravel under my feet, wishing to God I'd worn my gun that morning. With the Colt, all you had to usually do was show it and folks got peaceable. I left the trunk lid open to block Rebecca off from whoever came up behind. We'd raised a trail of dust and it stung my nose. The blue car turned off the highway and began cruising toward us. I wasn't too worried about a bottle of lye. He wouldn't slosh it at me, for fear of getting some on himself, and he wouldn't want to carry it up to a guy with a tire iron that might break it. And I couldn't see him setting out in the morning with a bottle of lye and a gun, both. Then I realized how dumb I was. If it was Halliday, he most likely carried a gun the way he carried a handkerchief. The big car coasted to a halt, glittering. It had been polished to within an inch of its life. The driver sat still for a moment, then got out. I was even dumber than I thought.

He reached back into the car and set a ten-gallon hat on his head. It was Lorin Shade.

I started laughing.

He walked halfway up to us, then stopped. "I didn't know it was you," he said. "I thought it was some fancy fella, in those clothes. You can put that iron down now. I guess you got the right to laugh. I guess it's laughable."

His eyes were steady, and so was his voice, but you could see what it cost to keep them that way. He was bitterly humiliated. At the sound of Shade's voice, Rebecca shot out of the car and stood staring, motionless. I put the tire iron away and closed the trunk. "Don't mind me, Shade," I said. "It's just nerves. You gave us a fright."

"I'm sorry," he said. Then he looked at Rebecca. That was worse than looking at me, but he managed it. "Hello, Becky. I'm awful sorry I worried you."

"What." She shook her head. "What."

"I know you're in trouble, Becky," he said. "I guess you kid about it sometimes, but I know it's bad. And I've been trying . . . I thought, if maybe I could just sort of quietly keep an eye. Just quietly. And, and they gimme some time at the Ever-Brite, and I know about, I guess I think about all these, these men you talk to, and, uh." He couldn't make it. He dropped his eyes. "I guess it's all no part of my business anyhow. I'm awful sorry for the trouble."

"All right, Lorrie," Rebecca said. "It's all right."

"I'm sorry, Becky."

"Go home, Lorrie," she said, eyes closed. "Just . . . go . . . home."

Shade nodded, and then nodded at me, and then walked, a little jerkily, back to his car. It was an old Buick, not a new Lincoln. It was awfully shiny, though. He backed up all the way down to the highway, and then we watched him turn and head south.

Rebecca began to tremble. Her arms hung limp at her sides, but her hands were in fists, and the tremors started small and then got bigger, until it seemed someone angry was shaking her. I put my arms around her, and she set both hands flat on my chest and stared at them, then slipped her arms under my jacket and hugged me tight around the waist, mashing her face against me. The shuddering almost shook both of us. It went on for a little while. Then she grew still, gradually, and then she leaned back and looked wonderingly up at me. I lay my hand on her cheek and her eyes closed. I smelled the eucalyptus, and the chaparral all around us. I lowered my face slowly toward hers. Her lips parted and she let her head sink back luxuriously.

When our mouths were an inch apart, I whispered: "You're a goddamn liar."

She tried to jerk away.

"You're a liar," I said. "Maybe it's not even your fault. You were probably born that way, but you'd think you'd be better at it by now. I called Ciro's yesterday. They never heard of you."

"What? I—"

"Why lie about a little thing like that, unless the whole thing was a fairy tale?"

"I used a different—"

"Why use a false name to take a job as a hat check girl?"

"Let *go* of me."

"It's okay. I lied too. I never called Ciro's."

"Please, I can't—"

"Think straight, sure. That's why we're talking now, because when you think, you lie. How much of that story was true?"

"He's going to *burn* me. Let me *go*."

"What's up between you and Lance Halliday?"

"He's going to burn me."

"Why?"

"Let me—"

"Why?"

"Because I stole his money!" she screamed into my face. *"I stole his goddamn money!"*

I let go of her and stepped back.

"There," I said, "that wasn't so bad, was it?"

She pushed herself upright with a hand on the fender, and stood there with her eyes closed, breathing.

"Keep going," I said. "Why'd you steal from him? Don't think. Tell."

"Because I had the chance to," she said. "Because he'd, because I had been in a movie for him. Two movies. I lied when I said it wasn't him. And, afterward . . . And I did sleep with him. He always has them himself, afterward. Has us. He, you've met him, he's very charming, and treats you like, like you were a real actress. And makes you think you're being very brave and glamorous, even, and that everyone else is just stuffy, and that you're just the most beautiful thing. I can't help how stupid that sounds. It's true that I fell for him. That part was true. And it was only after, when he was lying there, half asleep, it's as if I didn't know until then how much he'd taken from me. I had to get out of the room. He keeps this woman's dressing gown in his closet. For whoever, you know. I put on the gown and slipped out of the room, just to be away from him and think, and he'd left his jacket in the living room, on that flowered armchair there. And there was a pocket in the dressing gown. I think that's what gave me the idea. I just picked up the jacket and took out his wallet and took the money from it and put it in the pocket of the gown. Because if he was going to take from me . . . And my purse was on the dining room table, and my shoes were by the sofa, so I just kept going. I knew it would take him a while to see I'd gone, because my clothes were all on the floor of his room, but I didn't want to see any of those clothes again, and I drove home in the shoes and dressing gown, just like that. I knew there was a lot of money, but I didn't know until I got home that there was nearly fourteen hundred dollars. It must have been money he'd gotten to pay us all."

"When did he threaten you?"

"Right away. I'd gotten back to my room, and then the landlady knocked on my door, and I thought maybe she'd seen me coming home like that after all, but what she had to say is that there was a phone call for me, from my—" She laughed briefly. "From my brother. And he was sorry to call so late, but it was an emergency. And I got on, and he said, *You have a pretty face.* He told me to keep the money, because I'd need it, and then he told me what he was going to do."

"Did you actually meet him at Ciro's?"

"No. He knows where to find girls like me."

"When'd you take the photos? The photo-booth photos."

"That was the way I told you. He did take me out and try to show me a good time. After. And then we went back to his house. He likes to think the girls he hires are really his."

"You were smiling pretty good in the picture."

"I wanted to be having a good time. Don't you ever do that? Smile when you wish you were enjoying yourself?"

"Maybe I ought to try it. Where's that fourteen hundred?"

She flushed. "I gave you everything that's left of it."

"What did you do with the rest?"

"I, ah. I thought it would be better if it was more."

I started laughing again. "You took it out to the track and lost it."

"No," she said. "I can't look at you and— No. It was poker. I really am pretty good at cards, like Lorrie said. But not that night."

I was laughing, shaking my head.

She began to smile herself, shakily. "I had a system, you know. I had it worked out."

"Sure. You know how many times I've had it all worked out?"

"Yes," she said, laughing shakily. "I believe I do." She stopped and gave me a little punch in the chest, then hit me there hard. "Someday," she said fiercely, "I hope somebody about ten feet tall comes along and bends *you* over backward that way."

"It's been tried."

"Well. Well, at least you brush your teeth."

"I know. I was thinking it would've been better if I'd eaten some garlic."

"How did you know I was lying?"

"Because you're a liar."

"So it wasn't anything I said today, or that Shade was here?"

"No. I always knew you must be lying about at least some of this. Shade shook you up, and I thought I saw a chance to squeeze a little truth out."

"You saw a chance . . . And here I was calling you nice. I suppose you can be, but you're also somewhat horrible, aren't you?"

"Anyway, this story's better than the first."

"Thanks. Well, I guess I'll drop you home now."

"Thanks."

"I guess I've brought all this on myself."

"That's right. From now on, don't lie to me. It makes everything harder."

"From now on?" she said. "You'll still help me?"

"Sure."

"Even now?"

"I took your money."

"It was stolen."

I said, "Most money is."

15
Two Dozen Roses

As soon as Rebecca dropped me off, I got into my car and went to a florist. There was a young gal at the counter and a middle-aged woman in back. I asked to talk to the older woman. She set down her shears and came to the counter, peeling off her gloves. I said my wife was mad at me and what did she suggest? I left with two dozen pink roses in a pink vase with gold doodads and drove over to Republic, holding it between my knees. Mattie Reece's feet were back on the desk when I came in. I set the roses down next to them and dropped into a chair. He looked me over. I didn't seem to please him much.

"You bringing me flowers, soldier?" he said.

I shook my head. "You're bringing your wife flowers."

"Why?"

"Because she's mad at you."

"Why would she be mad?"

"She's married to you."

He nodded. "Thanks for the flowers. Still waiting to hear on Halliday. Couple days."

"Appreciate it," I said.

He pointed his chin at my suit. "Going to a fancy dress ball?"

"Lenny Scarpa's taking me to the prom."

"Is he now."

"I work for him. As of last night."

"Huh. I thought you were working for your lulu."

"I am. By working for Scarpa."

He thought that over. He didn't enjoy it. Mattie drinks and chases, but he likes things to go right. He likes the law. I guess he wouldn't want that to get around. His feet were crossed left over right, and he recrossed them right over left, looking off into the corner.

He said, "Don't explain it to me, all right? I just hope to hell you know what you're doing."

"A man in a suit like this always knows what he's doing. Tell me something, Mattie. I'm an industry guy, and I want a little snow on my roof. Where do I go?"

"To your new boss," he said grimly.

"Where else?"

"Nowhere else."

"Think harder. Somebody's been cutting in on Scarpa's movie customers. Enough so he's hired some palooka to go hunting for him. At least, that's what I hear."

"You don't say." Reece's eyes got soft and happy. "Thanks. That's nice. That's nicer than flowers."

"Always happy to help, Mattie. Where do I buy my hop?"

There was a battered clothbound address book on the corner of his desk. He worked his mouth around a little, then shoved the book toward me with the heel of his shoe. "Look up *Paley*," he said. "With a *P*."

I opened the book and began leafing through the *P*s.

"Movie people aren't like your regular doper," Mattie said, "Your regular doper's a working joe. He's got someone down on the shop floor, say, and they go out for a smoke and do the buy on the loading dock and hurry back before break's over, because they've got sandwiches to finish. Well, I guess some movie people'll do that, gaffers and so forth, but mostly movie people like everything to be fun. And they get their stuff at parties. Any given time, there's two three dope parties going in this town, just for folks in the business. They move around a lot, close down and open up again, but you tend to see the same folks setting out the onion dip. Thing is, a new one's popped up just in the last few weeks, and nobody knows who's behind it. Runs most nights at the old Paley place."

"Nita Paley," I read aloud. "1625 Marine Street, Santa Monica."

"That's it."

"Nita Paley. Didn't she used to do Gypsy types? For Griffith and so on."

"That's the one. Great big spooky black eyes. Ohio farm girl."

"She must be getting on."

"Drowned in '46 off Malibu. Nance Altschuler bought the place four years ago when her folks finally kicked her out. She and her artistic friends played house there a while, but what goes on these days is a little too rank even for Miss Altschuler and I hear she don't show so much anymore. Her friends do, though. Nancy's got friends."

"Who goes to that sort of place?"

"Different kinds. Not just hopheads, either. The thing's supposed to be some kind of art bit, with these sculptors and so forth that come around, probably for the food, and also you got that little element of, ah, danger I guess is how they think of it, and so everybody in the business who likes to feel they're a little bohemian or little dangerous thinks it's cute to come by and have a few drinks with the dope fiends. And also, you get to show your date how connected you are, because they run the place like an old speak, with a hard boy on the door, and nobody gets in without somebody's okay."

"I think I can manage that," I said, standing. I pushed his foot over and set the address book back where it'd been. "Thanks, Mattie."

"I liked your old clothes better," he said, looking off into the corner again. "These kind of have a smell."

"You get used to it," I said. "I'll call you."

"You see any of my people there, give 'em my love."

"Buy me a suit and we'll talk about it," I said, and went out.

I stopped in the outer office, perched on the corner of an empty desk, and looked at my watch. Four o'clock. Lisa Rae Bellinger would still be at the Gollar Agency. I picked up a phone. "It's the gumshoe," I said, when she came on the line.

"Hello, Gumshoe," she said. "You called after all. Did somebody show you how to use a telephone?"

"I went down to the library and got a book on the subject."

"Someone taught you to read?"

"It had pictures. Want to go to a party tonight?"

"Why, how very nice. You're taking me to a party."

"No," I said. "You're taking me."

Lisa Rae Bellinger was a skinny little thing, but what she ate was prime rib and peas, and what she drank was champagne, and where she did it was Musso & Frank's, and how I knew is, she told me so as soon as she got in the car at eight. Then I took her there and she demonstrated. She wore a steel-blue pleated dress with one of those three-inch patent leather belts you use to show how little your waist is. She looked awfully nice when she was eating, and just as nice when I was following her out to the car. When I pulled up in front of 1625 Marine she still looked nice, but she didn't look happy anymore. It had been a pretty house once, a rambling brick one-story with a winding flagstone walk and a couple big mullioned bay windows, but the shutters needed paint and the weeds were coming up between the flagstones and waist-high in the flowerbeds. There were cars parked all over what was left of the lawn. "Where are we," she said.

"Nita Paley used to live here."

"Uh huh," she said slowly. "Uh . . . huh."

"I guess you've heard about this place."

"I guess I have."

"You're not a china doll, Miss Bellinger, or I didn't think you were. But I can run you home now if you'd rather."

"Do you know, Mr. Corson, do you know how foolish I can be? Why, when you called me up this afternoon, I actually permitted myself to imagine you weren't just working."

"I am working," I said. "I'm not just working."

"That's a little subtle for me."

"I'm sorry. I need in over there. You know people and you're a looker. They'd be happier to see you than me. I'd like to see you myself some night when I'm not working, but this is a working night."

"Does it have to be?"

"Yeah."

"How come?"

"Because you can't do the work when it suits you. You've got to do it when they give it to you."

"Ain't that the truth," she said. "Well. I s'pose this is the sort of thing a girl should see at least once in her life. Like the Grand Canyon."

"I can run you home now if you'd rather. I'll find another way in."

"No. No, I believe my curiosity's getting the better of me."

"Lucky curiosity."

"Tomorrow, Mr. Corson, you can go back to the library and get a book on manners. With pictures. I imagine that's a parking spot over there."

The fellow on the door was wide enough that if you had to walk all the way around him you'd be tired. They'd brought out a bar stool for him to sit on. He was sort of half-sitting on it with one foot on the ground in case he had to move quick. He looked comfortable, like he was used to sitting that way. He wore a black turtleneck, old khaki slacks, and the kind of big straw hat you usually see on a horse. He watched us come up the walk as if he thought we might not be the Royal Couple, but he was polite enough when he said, "Sorry, friends. Private party."

"Oh," Lisa Rae said, "but we're *very* private people."

"Wish I could help you," he told her, sounding like he meant it.

He was enjoying looking at her.

"Dear me how mortifyin'," Lisa Rae said. "And here I thought I was *expected*."

"Expected by . . . ?"

"If Grammy's arrived, would you mind awfully much telling him that Lisa Rae's out waitin' on the front walk?"

"Mr. Neale's expecting you?"

"If he can still recall what he expects," she said

sweetly. "It's early enough in the evenin' for that, wouldn't you think?"

The doorman considered, then reached out a big arm and opened the door for us. "Beg your pardon, Miss Bellinger," he said. "But I'm sure you understand. Mr. Neale hasn't been by yet this evening. I'll tell him you're here when he comes."

"Oh, I'm Miss Bellinger now, am I?" she said.

"You wouldn't remember, but last fall you told me my face was too round to play gladiators."

"Well, come by the office sometime, cuz, and I'll be happy to forget you again."

"It's a date," he said affably as we went by.

The door opened into a living room. It was a big square room and looked bigger because it was half-empty. There were two sofas, and someone had taken the legs off one of them so it sat right on the floor. A young man in a Hawaiian shirt and shorts was asleep on it face-down, a beach towel wrapped around his legs. There was an enormous fireplace on the far wall with two racing bicycles in it instead of logs. There were a couple big paintings on the wall with no frames, but they were long-hair stuff that didn't look like anything and you'll have to ask someone else about them. There was a hi-fi in the corner, a good one, and piles of records on the floor and leaning up against the wall, and a trim gray-haired man in a blue blazer was down on one knee, going through the records with a disappointed look. I said, "Graham Neale comes here?"

"It's the sort of place he'd be. He's a sorry critter. Well, Mr. Corson, here you are like you wanted. Have I earned my dinner yet, or do you want Mr. Neale's autograph, too?"

I shook my head. "Can it. It's the doorman's job to be bitched at. It isn't mine. I asked you, in or out. You said in."

"Well," she said.

"Can it. I don't want to have your moping all night on top of everything else."

She squinched her eyes and put up her pointy little fists. She held the pose, looking mean.

"Well I'm damned. You pulled my file," I said.

She dropped her fists and nodded, grinning. She looked almost embarrassed. "That's right, Rocky Marciano. I read your file."

"I'll be goddamned," I said. "I'd thought all that'd be thrown away by now."

"Ollie never throws anything aw   " she said. "That's why he's rich."

"I'll be goddamned."

"I do apologize, Mr. Corson. I hate a mopey girl too. I hate a girl who says, oh, maybe I will and maybe I won't, but remember, whatever happens'll be all your fault. And now I will behave. And become a perfect delight. So. What brings the great gumshoe and his girl assistant to this low haunt?"

"Dope."

"My my. I'd say we came to the right place."

"I want to know who supplies this party. Not the people who sell here, but the man they get it from."

"That's easy enough. Lenny Scarpa, or one of his fellas."

"No. Somebody new."

"Says who?"

"Says Scarpa."

"My my my."

"Guess we're a little early, though. It'll be better when there's more people and they're drunker."

"We're way too early, Mr. Corson. It's not even ten-thirty. If you'd asked me I could've told you that, and we could've gone someplace nice a couple hours first and I could've taught you to dance."

"What makes you think I can't dance?"

"I don't care if you can. I like teaching you things."

Behind us, the man in the blazer must have found something he approved of, because the hi-fi let out a big blat of music, and then he adjusted the volume and a bossa nova started playing. He stood up and did a few steps by himself, nodding. He had a little bristly mustache. He was good.

Lisa Rae took my arm and said, "Let's go see what we can see."

16

Gold Clouds

The dining room was the old-fashioned long kind, with sideboards. There was a sort of buffet laid out on the table, or what was left of one. Some of it looked like it had been there yesterday. We went out the French doors at the back and were on a flagstone patio around a big pool. Around it a few people were chatting listlessly, dressed all different ways. The pool was half-empty, the deep end full of black water and leaves. They'd set up a bar with a guy in a white coat next to the pool and put a record player on the diving board with an extension cord running back to the house. It was playing Chubby Checker and two couples were dancing down on the bottom of the pool at the shallow end, where it was dry. They didn't seem to be having a big time. They looked like they were doing it so they could say they'd been to a dope party and danced in the pool. Lisa Rae and I got drinks and went through a door on the other side of the

pool to what must have been called the sun room. There
was a piano there and a folding chair, and the guy in the
folding chair was reading the paper. He didn't look up.
There were five bedrooms, three of them empty, one of
them locked, and one full of reef smoke and a card game.
They didn't look up, either. In the corner there was a big
circular tray of sugar cookies. Lisa Rae ate three with a
look of great concentration.

"This is no good at all," she said. "We're just sailing
through here like the Seventh Fleet, and much too nice
dressed. Everybody just stops what they're saying and
watches us sail on by."

"Let's split up," I said.

"Yes," she said. "That's exactly what we should do. I'll
go off somewhere and make all the men think I like
them, and you go find some girls and make them think
you like them. And we'll meet back here around midnight and see what we've got."

I said that sounded fine and she headed for the living
room and I went out back to the pool. The party was
beginning to pick up. I walked past Dorothy Tremaine
and almost didn't recognize her. She was wearing big
black-framed glasses and a baggy black sweater and tore-
ador pants. She played wisecracking secretaries and I was
surprised how young she was. I didn't try to talk to her.
She looked like she thought she was incognito. I saw a
driver I knew from Republic and we gave each other the
raised eyebrows and then chatted awhile, but he was just
there to drink and chase kittens, or so he said. I saw a
couple more people about as well-known as Neale and
Tremaine, and some players who were just half-familiar
faces, but you couldn't think what they'd done, and some
gaudy specimens who must have been choreographers or
designers, and some set dressers and grips and a couple
guys who might've been artists, the new kind, that try to

look like dockworkers. People were beginning to get just-nicely, and I thought I might find a loose thread to pull on pretty soon if I kept my wits about me this time. I'd finished my drink, a short gin, and I thought I'd go fill the glass up with water somewhere so I'd look like I was still drinking. The kitchen wasn't anyplace obvious, because when they built this house, that was somewhere only ser-vants went, so I worked my way toward the back and finally found it past a maid's room and a little swinging door. There was a woman in there wearing not much and holding a knife. "Do you want a sandwich," she said.

I said I did.

Her face was broad across the brow and cheekbones, young and coarsely pretty, with a turned-up nose and fine-grained pink skin. She had a nice shape and plenty of it. In a few years she'd have more than she wanted. Her nails were gnawed short, with little bits of flaked-off red polish on them, and she wore a satin kimono pat-terned with dragons and gold clouds, which she wasn't too fussy about keeping closed in front. There was a big stack of sandwiches at her elbow. She seemed to like making them. She didn't offer me one of the sandwiches in the pile. She took a loaf and sawed off a couple fresh slices. She made them a little thicker than the others. She set them side by side like it was important where they went, then looked over the cheeses and meats she'd set out on the counter, knife poised, drumming the fingers of her plump left hand thoughtfully on the cutting board. "How's Miss Godalmighty?" she said absently.

"Who?"

"Your date. Miss High and Godalmighty Bellinger."

"Oh. Fine, thanks. She sends her love."

"You like tomatoes? Some people are allergic, but I think they're good."

"I like tomatoes."

"What she probably likes is you're not an actor."

"That's it."

"I guess she's not too high and mighty for a place like this."

"I guess she isn't. What did she turn you down for?"

"What?"

"I said, what did she turn you down for? Or did she just turn you down, period?"

The girl in the kimono didn't say anything, just kept slicing tomatoes.

"Me, I'd cast you in a minute," I said. "Lucrezia Borgia. Salome. Medea. Of course, you might have to put some clothes on."

"Most guys wouldn't complain. Clothes're just a bourgeois convention anyway. You look really silly, all got up like that." She pointed the big knife at my nose. "You're teasing me," she said with satisfaction.

"Careful with that knife."

She laughed and flicked it at the ceiling. It whirled end over end, a rising, glittering circle of steel, and she caught it easily by the handle as it fell. "I don't have to be careful with knives," she said, suddenly cheery. "Anymore there's none of the good salami left, but this ham's pretty nice."

"That'll be fine."

She began shaving off slices of ham. She had that kitchen all set up the way she wanted it. She went with the house, all right. "Friend of Nancy's?" I said.

"That girl doesn't know who her friends are."

"No?"

"She's gotten very bourgeois. Anymore I'm the only one'll tell her the truth, and she doesn't like that. Oh, no."

"What's your name?" I said.

"Maddy."

"Maddy what?"

"Maddy nothing."

"Do you want to know my name?"

"I know your name. You're Suit Man. Having a good time tonight?"

"Sure."

"How come you're not having a good time?"

"Do you always disbelieve what people tell you?"

"Mostly. Don't you think that's a good idea?"

"Yeah, actually."

"I think we're having a good party tonight. How come you're not enjoying it?"

"Oh, I dunno. Doesn't seem like it's really gotten cooking yet."

"Oh. Well, he'll be in later."

"Who will?"

"I told you, later."

The sandwich was finished. She took a big bite and began chewing. I said, "Wasn't that going to be my sandwich?"

"You didn't really want it," she said with her mouth full.

"You know, you're right," I said, and went out to find Miss Godalmighty.

Lisa Rae was in the glassed-in gallery that ran along one side of the pool, talking to Graham Neale. He was standing in a pose he'd made slightly famous: hands in his pockets, feet planted, looking solid and bluff and reliable. He was smiling down on Lisa Rae like a doting uncle, but his face was blotchy and damp-looking and there didn't seem to be much behind the smile. Ten years ago Neale had been a popular second lead. He was the guy in the bomber crew who died big in the last reel and the hero avenged him, or he'd lose the girl to the hero and have the rueful closing line as the hero and the girl strolled off together. He'd lost more girls than anyone else in pictures. He held the record. He looked up and saw me looking, and then Lisa Rae turned and smiled. She patted his cheek and said something and trotted over to me, and Neale grinned at me and turned to amble off.

"Did you make all the girls think you liked them?" she asked, tapping a forefinger against my tie and smiling.

She'd gotten a bit of glow on.

"Knocked 'em down like ninepins," I said.

"He's coming by later," she reported.

"So I heard. Who's coming by later?"

"The fella you're looking for."

"Right. What's his name?"

"Nobody wanted to say much if I didn't already know."

"That's okay."

"I guess this sleuth stuff's harder than I thought."

"Well, they didn't want to tell me, either. Neale wouldn't say?"

"I'm the last person Grammy'd tell. The very last. He loves me, he truly does, but tonight he hates me. Because I caught him in a place like this and wasn't surprised."

"I can see where that might sting."

"So I don't have much information for you. Are you very disappointed in me, Mr. Corson? Now, what're you smiling about?"

"You pulled my file," I said.

"I did. How come that surprises you?"

"I'm surprised you thought to do it."

"Why? I've been thinking about you, Mr. Corson."

"Nice things, I hope?"

She shook her head. Our faces were very near now.

"Bad ideas," she murmured. "I get the worst ideas. The . . . worst."

I kissed her. She was gripping my lapels, hanging on. After a while we stopped kissing.

"Lisa Rae," I said. A little tendril of hair had come loose, and I tucked it back where it belonged.

She took my nose between her thumb and forefinger and tried to straighten it out, and then she poked a little here and there at my face, and all the time her lips were moving around like they were remembering kissing me. She poked at my cheek.

"Missed a spot," she whispered.

"No I didn't."

"I guess you didn't. I guess you're one of these fellas who it doesn't matter how much they shave, they still look like they need to."

"Yep."

"I guess you're one of these fellas who doesn't look so smooth but gets girls anyhow."

"That's right."

"You've got lots of girls, huh?"

"No. I've been on my own awhile."

"I'm trying to decide, Mr. Corson, whether I'm stupid enough to have a little flutter with you. If you were a gentleman, you'd help me decide."

I kissed her again. She had her hands against my chest, her fingers stiff and a little clawed, and her elbows between my belly and hers, holding us just a bit apart, and was doing all her kissing with her mouth. I closed my eyes and didn't think about anything. I was happy. I could feel her back under my hands, tensing and relaxing again like a cat's will when you stroke it. This time she was the one who stopped. We examined each other.

"No . . . " she said.

"No?"

"No."

"Not stupid enough?"

"Plenty stupid enough. Plen-ty. But you lied to me, Mr. Corson."

"What about?"

"You told me there wasn't anybody else."

"I don't have anyone else."

"Oh no. There's someone, all right. Maybe you don't, um, have her yet. But I can see her in there, Mr. Corson. I can taste her."

"I don't have anyone else."

"And I'll tell you something about that girl, Mr. Corson. Whoever she is. She's just like me, Mr. Corson. All her ideas are bad. I believe I'll have Graham run me home now."

"I wish you wouldn't," I said.

"It's past his bedtime anyway. Good night, Mr. Corson."

She turned and walked off. I shut my mouth and watched her go. She went down the gallery, and I could see her through the glass, and then she turned again and I couldn't.

"He's a fairy, you know," said Maddy behind me.

I turned. Maddy was in the corner, propping up the wall with her broad soft back and finishing her sandwich.

"He's a big fairy. Grammy is," she said. "How's it feel, having a fairy beat your time?"

"You'll get fat," I told her savagely. "You are getting fat. And the sooner the better. I don't like you."

She picked a crumb off her front and ate it. "I'm sorry Miss Godalmighty gave you the air. You deserve her. You deserve each other. Why don't you go home, Suit Man? I don't see why you're here in the first place. You don't fit in. You're not having any fun. You're just making everybody uncomfortable who's here to enjoy theirself. What do you want here, anyway?"

"Dope," I snapped.

"Well, that's easy enough," she said, swallowing the last bit and licking her thumb. "Come on."

She boosted herself off the wall with a shove of her rump and set off down the hallway without looking around. I followed her. We crossed the dining room and she led me along the other wing of the house into a woman's bedroom, very untidy. Out the window was a dry fountain with a figure of a faun playing a double flute. "Come into my parlor, like they say," she said over her shoulder. "Close the door."

As she spoke, she was undoing the sash of her robe. She pivoted gracefully as it fell open and stood facing me, waiting for a trumpet flourish. Underneath, she wore peach satin drawers and a smudgy yellow garter. She looked like two dozen roses in a pink pot. I closed the door. She ran two fingers along the elastic of her drawers, slipped them inside just over her left hip, drew out a packet folded from patterned gold paper, and held it up. "You fuss around more'n you need to, Suit Man. Some things're easy."

"Not that easy," I said. "It's been a while since I bought any talcum powder. I'd like it to be a longer while."

She nodded, took a short flat knife from under her garter, and flipped open the packet at one end with the tip of it, deft as a baccarat dealer turning a card. She slipped the knife inside and drew out a little mound of the powder, and held it in front of my face. Her hand didn't shake. I've known a few sleigh-riders and maybe that's why I was never interested enough in the stuff to try any. Anyway, I never had. I lowered my nose toward the knife, pressed my right nostril shut with my forefinger the way I'd seen it done, and snorted the cocaine up the left, praying I wouldn't sneeze.

It bit into my head with cold teeth. For a moment I held still, feeling something like pain behind my eyes. Then the gold clouds in Maddy's kimono seemed to swell, or maybe they just got very important-looking.

Everything in the room looked very clear and important. I was most important of all. I was King Barracuda. Maddy was very beautiful and mysterious. The back of my tongue was bitter as lye. "Good?" she said.

I nodded, and she closed up the packet and put it in my hand. It was warm. I hefted it and tried to look judicious. "Quarter-plate?" I said.

When I spoke, my lungs felt cold.

"That's right," she said. She licked the knife clean and tucked it away. "Full measure. Twenty bucks."

"How much more you got?" I said.

Her expression didn't change. I opened my wallet and held it out to her. She glanced inside, then pulled two packets from her left hip, one from her right, and began rummaging around behind her, looking at the ceiling. "I sewed the pockets in back too deep," she said. She got out one more and set them all in a row before me. "That's what's left tonight," she said. "Like I said, it's been a nice party."

"I was thinking more of fifty than five," I said.

She took back the four sealed packets and stowed them away beneath her tummy, and nodded at the one in my hand. "You tasted that and it was good, so you're buying it. For the rest, you'll have to talk to Billy when he gets here."

I gave her a twenty and said, "When'll that be?"

"When he wants," she said, stowing the bill where she'd stowed the merchandise. "People wait for Billy long's they have to."

She was murmuring, but I couldn't see why she had to talk so loud. I thought it might be a good idea to bust her one in that little nose. Or maybe marry her. They were both brilliant ideas. I felt like I could pick up the house and throw it if I wanted. It was an unrestful way to feel.

"Close that robe before I fall in love," I said, and went

back into the dining room.

After that, all I had to do was kill time. It didn't die without a struggle. I went back out to the pool and had a couple more drinks and then took another stroll through the dining room. Maddy had finally put out that stack of sandwiches. I had one. It was delicious. But in the middle it began to seem very strange to go around putting things in your mouth and chewing them, and I left the rest of it on the mantelpiece and tried playing the piano in the sun room. I've never learned how, but it seemed worth a try. Outside, someone bounced on the diving board for a joke so that the record player fell into the pool in the middle of a song. I thought that was pretty funny. I saw a door I hadn't noticed and went down some stairs. There was a long drab room down there with padding on the ceiling and side walls, and I remembered that Nita Paley had built an underground shooting range for some reason, but what they kept down there now was a pool table and a couple of busted easy chairs and some drunks, and I began playing pool for money. The first game, I wanted to jog around the table between shots. But by the second game I started coming out from under the powder, and soon I was thirty-two bucks up and the guy wanted double or nothing again. We were well along toward my sixty-four bucks when a thin man stepped up to my opponent and held out his hand for the cue. He nodded to him and to me and began to play.

He pocketed the first ball as if he was trying to get it out of the way so we could move on to something interesting, and then he sank another the same way. He chalked up sparingly and made two more. He was running the table, all right. I rested the butt of my cue on the floor and studied him. He held his shoulders high and wore his black hair slicked straight back. He would have been a handsome man if the bones of his face hadn't been a little too big and the skin over them too tight. His wore narrow gray boots with heels, tight black trousers that buttoned up the front and had no belt-loops, a yellow shirt, a bolo tie, and a charcoal gray jacket, cut short, like a bolero jacket. All of his clothes looked as if he'd spent money to have them made that way on purpose. He was a real desperado. He looked as much like Zorro as anyone could look who didn't have a sword and a flat black hat. Most coke hounds blink like fury, but he blinked only once in a while, slowly and sort of precisely, like a falcon. I wondered how much hop you had to run through to get that way. It wasn't hurting his game any. He sank the white with no more fuss than the other balls and laid his cue gently on the felt. I opened my wallet, counted out thirty-two dollars, and added it to the thirty-two on the edge of the table. Without taking his eyes from mine, he picked it up and held it off to the side. The other man I'd been playing said, "Well— Well, thanks, Billy," and put it in his pocket.

"Now we been introduced," Billy said.

17

Metz

He led me back out to the pool. There were twice as many people out there as I'd seen at midnight. Someone had lit the patio torches and turned off the colored floodlights, and all you could see was shadows. When the shadows talked they looked like they were conspiring, and when they danced they looked like black flames. Billy led me to a bench by a fitted fieldstone wall that ran along the back of the property. We sat and watched the dancers. "Pretty good brawl, huh?" he said.

"I've seen worse," I said.

"You're looking for two three pounds."

"No."

"That's what Maddy said. Her hearing's usually pretty good."

"That's what I told her. I came to talk to you, Billy, not your women. My name's Rose."

"Yeah? That the punch line?"

"Jesus, what're they teaching you kids these days? Stu Rose."

"I never heard of you."

I shook my head, amused. "Well, let's just say if you were running this luau anywhere up the Valley, you'd've heard of me a while ago."

"Yeah? Well, we're not up the Valley, dad, and you're not buying, you say. So what's the grift?"

"You picked an interesting spot, Billy. Right in Scarpa's back garden. Or haven't you heard of Lenny Scarpa either?"

"I hear way too goddamn much about Lenny Scarpa. You and him good buddies?"

"No," I said truthfully.

"I'm not a sociable boy, dad. Why're we talking?"

"Maybe we've got nothing to talk about," I said. "Maybe you've got all the supply you want. All the organization you want. Maybe you're never short of kale when you get a shot at a nice score. Maybe you want to stay small forever."

"You raise a lot of dust, don't you, daddy?"

"Talk English. And wipe your upper lip."

He didn't wipe it, but he had to stop himself.

I said, "I'm on your patch now, so I guess I'll let you call me daddy once in a while. But your patch ends where the driveway does. And at high tide my patch might slop

right over yours. Why don't we try a little manners and
see how it goes?"

He didn't say anything. We watched the dancers.

"You're Billy Metz," I said.

"Who'd you think I was?"

"All I knew was Billy, but I make you now. William R.
Metz. Production design at Paramount. You were really
up there for a while. They bounced you last fall and
nobody liked to say why."

"I walked," he said.

"Catherine the Great's palace in *Scarlet Monarch*.
That big, ah, that kind of desert fortress in *A Sound of
Distant Drums*. Lemme think."

"I was there seven years, dad. I did a lot of stuff."

"You were good," I said. "Really good. I could do
something like that, I wouldn't fool with anything else."

"Time comes you get tired of drawing little pictures."

"We might agree on one thing, Billy. Scarpa's had it his
own way in Santa Monica an awful long time."

"I'm not looking to be adopted. I like it on my own."

"You're brand-new, son. Fresh out of the cellophane.
It doesn't work that way, not without a setup. You got to
come in with somebody. Why not me?"

"You talk a lot."

"I like to talk, don't you?"

Metz stood.

"Let's go somewhere," he said.

We walked toward the house. When we came through
the French doors, I looked around and said. "Gimme a
minute. Jesus, I should've dropped bread crumbs."

"One off each bedroom," he said, waving. "Take your
pick. I'll be out front."

I nodded and headed off down the hall. The first bedroom had some folks getting acquainted on the bed, but I
didn't feel like excusing myself and I kicked the heel of

his shoe. He looked around. "Out," I said, and they buttoned up and got out. I picked up the phone on the bedside table. It was past two in the morning. Scarpa answered on the first ring. "Yeah," he said.

"Where do you want him?" I said.

"Where are you?"

"Santa Monica."

He thought a moment. "There's a little park, just south of the pier, called Crescent or something. Right by the end of Pico, where it meets the water. Half an hour."

He hung up, and I went out to find Metz. He was at the front door, ready to go.

I'd spoken too soon. He had the hat, too.

We walked outside without a word. He nodded when he saw my car. "Nice ride," he said.

"There's a story behind it," I told him. "Tell you on the way. You know a place called Franco's, down by the pier?"

"No," he said. "I don't like bars."

I swung out the driveway and headed for Lincoln Boulevard. "It's a decent little shack, for after hours."

"I don't give a goddamn. You run the Valley, why're you driving this wreck?"

"Long story, Billy. Long story, but I don't mind telling."

"I mind listening. Look, let's just pull into the first place we see."

"You're a jumpy fella, Billy. You should sniff less and drink more. We're going to Franco's."

"I don't need to go to Franco's. What, the house give you a percentage?"

"It's a good place to talk."

"We're talking now."

"I want you to meet an associate of mine."

"Aw, hell," he said disgustedly, "you're one of Scarpa's

boys," and slipped his hand into his jacket.

You'd expect a powder hound to be quick, and he was, but quick doesn't mean good, and I had a hold on his right wrist by the time he'd got a hold on his iron. We were on Lincoln by then, doing maybe forty. I eased it up past fifty. I didn't want anybody getting giddy and jumping out. I could tell he had his finger on the trigger, but I wouldn't let him draw, so his finger wasn't much good to him unless he felt like shooting a chunk off his hip. I jammed my thumb in between the tendons in his wrist and started working it around. He let out a thin noise between his teeth. "I never broke a guy's wrist this way," I said. "Want me to try?"

He backhanded me a few times lefty in the face. It wasn't worth writing down in my diary. "You're a jumpy fella, Billy," I said again. "Let go the gun."

"You want to cool me, dad, you'll have to work for it," he hissed. He tried kicking me.

"He wants to talk, Billy."

"Sure, talk. That's why the old heap. You leave it in a field somewhere and me in the trunk."

"Let go the gun, Billy," I said, working my thumb around. He let go, and I pulled his gun out and leveled it at his knee. "He wants to talk. That means I can't kill you, but he won't mind a little hole in your leg. So simmer down."

"I know his talk."

I sighed. "Scarpa doesn't kill punks like you himself. He doesn't mow his own lawn, either. Why don't you use that thing under your hat? You set up shop on Scarpa's patch. You must've known it was coming one day, a talk or a bullet. If it was a bullet, I'd give it to you now and save myself some aggravation. So it's talk, and you ought to be glad you're getting a chance to."

He made me a brief recommendation.

"Manners, Billy," I said, and tapped him in the mouth with his gun. "Turn around and face me with your back to the door and your hands on your knees." He repeated his recommendation, then did what I said. "And if you start feeling frisky, remember I don't need the gun to make you wish you were playing dress-up in some other town."

I put his gun down in my lap and finally shifted into third. He made another recommendation. I was beginning to worry. For a guy who thought he was about to be killed, Metz was more petulant than anything else, like someone was trying to take his scooter away. I said, "You really have been tampering with yourself, haven't you, Billy? Listen. When we get there, try and straighten up. Don't talk to him like you're talking to me."

He was trying to get his hat level on his head again.

I said. "Billy. I'm serious. Don't talk to Scarpa like this."

"I talk like I want to," he said.

"Jesus. All right. Sure," I said. "Talk like you want to to Lenny Scarpa. I won't have to learn any new tricks. I already know how to use a shovel."

Scarpa's car was a dark green Maserati with wire-spoke wheels. It looked fast, and it must have been, because he was waiting in it when we pulled up. The park was on a little grassy bluff overlooking the sea. You could see the pier, half a mile up the beach, the minarets on the ballroom still lit up, even that late. I heard they'd turned it into a roller rink. In the daytime you wouldn't be able to see the sand for the colored umbrellas, but it was empty now and black, and the black waves moved over it and back again like the shuttle of a loom. "Don't open your door," I told Metz. "Crawl out mine, so I can cover you." He did what I said, holding his hat steady with one hand, and then I walked him around to the front of Scarpa's car, where we had a little privacy from the houses behind. "Lenny," I said, "this is Mr. William R. Metz, formerly of Paramount, currently doing business at 1625 Marine."

Scarpa looked him over, then lifted the hat off Metz's head, holding it with two fingers.

"No," he said, and tossed it away.

Metz went on staring into Scarpa's face.

"Hello, Billy," Scarpa said. "You know who I am."

"I know who you think you are," Metz said.

"You didn't tell me he was C'd to the eyes," Scarpa said to me.

"Did I need to?"

"I guess not. Okay, Billy. Listen, all right?"

"I'm not hurting you any," Metz said.

"Billy. Santa Monica's my town. You can't do like this in my town. You can't come into my store, and spread out your merchandise on my counter, and start selling. All right? So that's done, but I'll tell you what might happen. You managed to pry off a nice little bit of my business. I like a guy who goes after what he wants. I like him better if he can get it. Long's he's not too crazy. Long's he can be told. I can always use a good salesman in my store, Billy. Movie people buy from me, sure, but they'd like it a lot better buying from one of their own. So that could be nice for me, and I could make it nice for you, too. Better supply than you got right now, fewer worries. More business. Things go well, I could set you up in a shop of your own."

"I already got my own shop."

"No. Ten minutes ago you did. Now you don't. Billy, are you listening?"

"What else've I got to do, dad? You talk more'n your gorilla."

"He saw your gun, right?" Scarpa asked me.

"It's his gun," I said.

"If it's his gun, he ought to know what it does."

"It doesn't do a damn thing," Metz said. He'd stopped blinking and his eyes were steady as glass eyes. "Not here in the middle of all these houses, it doesn't, and I'm not worried about anything else you can do to me here. And I'll worry about what you do tomorrow tomorrow. You're telling me you want a war? Okay. It's war."

Scarpa was shaking his head.

"Billy—" I said.

"Less mouth," Scarpa told me. He turned back to Metz. "You got the wrong map, son, and no light to read it by."

"Your town," Metz said. "You coming around and telling me this is your town. Listen, ginzo. My people've been here since before they paved the roads. When they built that pier, my great-grand-uncle had six and a quarter percent of it. My father was Sandy Metz and if they had movies wherever you come from, you been looking at his costumes since you first stole a nickel for a ticket. We were in Hollywood before there was any such thing. Now, I don't know what your town is. Chicago, maybe, or Palermo, but it isn't here. It isn't here. This is my town. And maybe you can come into my town and tell me what I can and can't do, but you haven't proved it yet. All you've proved is, you can talk. And I'm done talking."

"You know, that's true," Scarpa said.

If I'd known what was coming, I still might not have been quick enough to stop it. There was a stiletto in Scarpa's right hand, as if it had always been there, the kind with hardly any handle to it, and while I was noticing it, Scarpa was swinging his left hand up and sinking his thumb and forefinger into the soft flesh under Metz's jaw. Metz's mouth popped open and Scarpa whipped the stiletto up and over and buried it in Metz's tongue, to the handle, rising up on his toes and falling back again in one movement, like a bullfighter. Metz dropped gagging to the grass. It was the kind of thing you half see and half figure out later. And then I was standing between them, facing Scarpa, and I think I was shaking my head no.

"Don't worry," Scarpa told me. "All done. You didn't used to be so delicate."

I looked back. Metz was on his knees, the blood streaming over his chin. He was trying to hold it in with his hands.

"Stop aside," Scarpa said gently. "I want to say good-night to our date."

I stepped aside, and Scarpa hunkered down next to Metz. Metz was trying to stick his fingers back in where the wound began and press it shut, and then gagging and coughing them out, then trying again. His yellow shirt was red. He'd rolled his eyes down, trying to see into his own mouth. He looked to be split open in there, right back to the root. Scarpa began wiping the stiletto clean on the grass. "You're done now, Billy," he said. "You were too snowed-in to hear a kind word. So you're out of the business. I got a little list of people who used to buy from me. They don't buy from me again in the next couple weeks, I'll come kill you. I ever hear you've sold anything to anyone else, anywhere, I'll kill you. I ever get bored and need cheering up, I'll kill you." He examined the knife, turning it in the moonlight, then stood and tucked it away in his jacket. Metz vomited through his fingers, and we both stepped back quickly. "You're done, Billy," Scarpa said, looking down at him. "Tell me you under-stand."

Metz nodded vigorously.

I took out my handkerchief and gave it to him. "Here," I said. "It's clean. Fold it in half and press it down on the wound, hard. Make it hurt. Go sit in my car.

I'll get you to the hospital."

Metz staggered to his feet, stuffing my handkerchief into his mouth. That was all he was going to do now, what someone told him.

Scarpa smiled faintly. "I didn't figure you for the Florence Nightingale type."

"You can bleed out through the tongue as easy as anyplace else," I said. "You want headlines? Dope King Sought in Tongue Slay?"

"What're you so wrought up about, anyway? You did good."

"I didn't do anything."

"Yeah, that's what was good."

"What do you think you taught him?" I said.

"Hell with what I taught him," Scarpa said. "It's what I taught *you*. I taught you you don't hurt 'em when you're angry. You hurt 'em when you're not angry."

"Uh huh. Where's my pay?"

"For a day's work? You're wearing it."

"Fair enough." I opened my wallet, took out seventy-one dollars and the gold packet and held it out to him.

"What's this?" he said.

"What's left of your expense money, and a bindle of Billy's dope."

He stared at it a moment, then said, "Thanks," and slipped it in his pocket. "You did good. Go on home. We'll have something else for you in a couple days."

I turned to go. Metz was leaning against my car, holding my handkerchief in with both hands.

"Ray," Scarpa said softly, and I stopped. "You got a look on your face. You're trying not to, but you do."

"What do you care what I look like, Lenny?"

"Oh, I care," he said. "I care. Cause now, Ray? Now you work for me."

18
Farmhouse

I'm not often up early, especially when I've been out that late the night before, but next morning I was awake, coldly awake, as soon as a little light seeped around the curtains. I lay there with my eyes closed, trying to convince myself I was still asleep. I'd had the kind of dreams you wake up from tired. I was trying not to think about the night before. I'd stopped the car at St. John's, watched Metz stagger through the emergency room doors, and taken off. When I got home, I'd brought a pan of water out to the car and washed off the seat and door and fender. Then I'd washed my own hands, twice, in water almost hot enough to blister, but this morning they still didn't feel clean. I guessed they weren't. I got out of bed and walked around the apartment, picking stuff up and putting it down again. There still wasn't a thing in the house, not even coffee. I didn't have much appetite anyway, so I showered, dressed, and read yesterday's papers until noon, when I went to meet Joanie from the probate office.

Joan Healey was the most generous and least worried person I knew. She was about thirty-five and looked ten years younger and acted like a high-school girl who'd just discovered malteds. I never figured out whether she thought she was ugly enough that she had to take what she could get or beautiful enough that she had a civic duty to spread it around, but she'd pretty much throw a leg over anybody who asked. Her boyfriends tended to be the kind of men you find with women like that. Her roommates stole from her. This interested her, the stealing, and she'd speculate about how they did it and how much they got. She was a big, soft-looking girl with energetic brown eyes, and she still trusted everybody she met and believed every story she heard. I was always glad to see Joanie, because it meant nobody had killed her yet.

I took her to the Gold Medal. She always had the fried chicken platter, and it never died a lingering death. Between bites, she said, "Honey, I feel so awful and I hope you won't be upset, but I couldn't find you hardly anything. Halliday's Halliday's legal name. I know it sounds phony but he could've changed it anywhere in the country and we wouldn't have the records. He bought the Shippie place in that name three years ago for thirteen five and he's *already* got a second mortgage on it. I'd love to have listened to him talk somebody into that one. The Lincoln's his, all right, but he's way behind on it. He's got two other nice cars, a Buick and a Studebaker, and he's way behind on them, and I've written them down with their license numbers, um, come on now, oh, *here*." She handed me a little scrap of paper with potato salad on the corner. "And he's been arrested twice for pandering, *and,* are you ready? The charges were dropped both times with no trial. Isn't that interesting?"

"How'd you get the pandering bit?"

"Oh, honey, I know so many cops, I could murder somebody every Tuesday and get off with a warning. Jay Russert, you know Jay? Well, he's not Organized but he is Vice, and he says they're *very* interested in your Mr. Halliday. Not because he does so much, but because he's all over the lot doing everything and he doesn't seem to have good sense."

"Joanie, this is terrific. You've really done a job for me."

"I haven't done hardly anything, and here's the worst. As far as L.A. County's concerned, there's no such thing as Rebecca LaFontaine at all. We don't have a thing on her, not a thing. I want you to tell me the truth about Miss LaFontaine."

"I'm in love with her, Joanie."

"I knew it. I knew it."

"I'm going to take her away from him. He's not good enough for her."

"I should say not. Is she really beautiful? Where did you meet?" Joanie settled in with her face in her palms and her eyes shining and for a while I said whatever came to mind. Joanie loved stories—she probably lived her life the way she did because she loved stories—but she didn't necessarily listen to them that closely.

After I settled the bill Joanie had a bit of a dilemma, since she couldn't take me to her new place, because she'd just moved way out to Baldwin Park and it was still all boxes and depressing, and she couldn't go back to my place because she needed to do some shopping while she was downtown. You could see her getting upset at the idea that an old friend like me might have to go home unbedded, but I reminded her that I was in love now and she lit up again. She gave me a five-minute goodbye kiss and said she'd have to have me over soon when she was settled, some afternoon or maybe some evening when Lewis, had I met Lewis? was on the late shift. Then she gave me a wave and headed off to Bullock's. If nobody killed Joanie she'd make someone a wonderful little wife.

When I got home I called Mattie Reece and asked if he had anything yet. He suggested I cultivate patience. He didn't use those words. I stretched out on the bed and looked at the ceiling for a while. Then I rolled over and looked at the blanket. I was supposed to sit tight and wait for Scarpa to call. He'd call when he had more work.

Work like last night's.

I went to the closet and looked over my new suit again.

Somehow there wasn't any blood on it. You'd think there would be.

I wandered around the place some more, then sat down at the desk. I took out four sheets of paper and marked them SCARPA, BURRI, HALLIDAY, and REBECCA. Then I got out a fifth and marked it METZ, but that was silly. Metz was done, and I crossed out METZ and wrote in THE SITUATION. I laid them out in a row and started noodling names and facts and connecting them with arrows and generally smoking my meerschaum and playing my violin. When evening came, what looked best was the business card I'd found in Halliday's desk, the one with no name on it. The address was way out in Calabasas, and I got in the car and went there.

It was mostly ranches and farms out there, and the place I wanted looked to be a regular old farmhouse in the middle of an orchard, but they'd knocked down the barn in back and instead there was a gravel parking lot with seven cars in it. On impulse I kept out of the lot and parked on the shoulder across the road from the front door, facing back toward town. The orchard stretched out in the dark around me, a working orchard from the look of it, grapefruit from the smell, but I guessed whoever used to live in the house had sold out to a bigger concern and someone else was farming it now. There wasn't another house within a mile. I chewed my lip a little, then took off my holster and gun and put them in the glove compartment. I got out of the car and went to ring the doorbell.

The door was opened by a thin woman of fifty or so in a party dress that showed too much of her and tried to push around what it didn't show. She smiled at me and said hello honey. I nodded and said hello back. Behind and to the side of her was what looked like an ordinary front parlor in somebody's house, except they'd set an antique writing desk facing the door. When I didn't say anything more, she turned and walked back to the desk and sat down behind it with her ankles gracefully crossed and her fingers laced and her nails gleaming. They were some nails. Her hair was done Kim Novak-style and blonde enough to hurt. You could have sterilized a cut by running your fingers through that hair. The desk had a fake marble top and ball-and-claw feet, and was open in front to show off her legs. Her arms and legs were smooth and young-looking, the way you'll see sometimes with women who earn a living by physical labor. She'd probably done her share of what I guessed went on upstairs, before she moved over to management, and whatever else you want to call it, it is hard labor. "Why, I don't think I know you, honey," she said.

"I don't think you do."

"I'm Miss Delores," she said. "How're you doing tonight?"

"I'm Bill Jones," I said. "Fine."

She thought about that and decided it was a joke. She laughed. It didn't bother her hair any. "Well, I think we can get you relaxed now after your hard day, Mr. Jones. How does that sound?"

I said it sounded fine. She asked me if I wanted a drink and I said I was fine, then changed my mind and said gin and lime. She tapped the little bell at her elbow. Off to my left was a small arched doorway that must have led to the kitchen, and I heard footsteps and the clack of dishes being washed. There'd be someone there to make food and do the laundry. Especially laundry, there'd be lots of that. A short dark man in a white shirt and black trousers appeared from the direction of the kitchen. Delores told him to get me a gin and lime and he went silently away. He came back almost at once and set the drink on the writing table without looking at me. The kitchen noises hadn't stopped. I guessed it was him and a wife to do the chores, with maybe a shack out in the yard where they lived. I picked up the drink and had a taste. It was strong.

On the desk was the kind of little photo album grand-parents carry around to show off their grandchildren. It had only seven pages inside, and on each was a full-length snapshot of a woman. Two of them were white, three were Mexican or Filipino, one was a Jap, and one was colored. Beneath each picture someone had written a name and three figures separated by asterisks: 9–° 15–° 25– or 12–° 18–° 40–. Each woman had been posed in a formal dress, standing in front of the same pine-paneled wall. One plump brown girl wore what looked like a com-munion dress someone had gone over with scissors and thread, scooping out the neckline and splitting it up the side. She was coming out of it like toothpaste from a tube. Her name was Estrella and her rates were ten, six-teen, and thirty.

"A *very* good girl," Miss Delores said. "Especially when she has a gentleman to make her behave."

"Uh huh?" I said.

"Uh huh," she said.

"She looks young," I said.

Miss Delores leaned closer and murmured, "Only fif-teen."

"Is that right."

"You're shy," she said. "But there's no need to be shy." There was a small bakelite tray at her elbow, and she nudged it forward with a fingernail. I put two fives into it and she looked disappointed, then smiled. "You'll want more," she said, and tapped the bell again, twice.

"What do I owe for the drink?" I said.

"Oh," she said, "let's leave it on the tab for now.

Because I do believe Mr. Jones will be wanting more."

"Thanks," I said.

I heard heavy footsteps and a young man in a blazer came down the stairs. He had muscles and big shiny movie-star eyes, but his face was too short. It was like the face of a chisel, sloping down fast toward a sharp flat chin, with just a little slot of a mouth right above it. He was the kind of guy whose chest hair grows right up his neck. So am I, but I keep my shirt buttoned, and when I wear a gun I don't let it bulge out all over the place.

His eyes flicked down on the book of photos and he said, "Good to meet you, buddy. You're in luck, as it happens. Estrella's free. She's waiting for you."

I went to tip back my drink.

"No, no, take the drink, take the drink. We got coasters in the rooms."

I followed him up the stairs, holding my drink. It was just an old farmhouse up there. A big farm family had lived here once. It was silly to let that throw me. The world was full of whorehouses, and most of them had been something else first. Then I saw what had been bothering me.

There was a new Yale lock on every one of the upstairs doors.

The pimp got out a ring of keys, opened one of the doors, and motioned me inside. "Here you go," he said. "I'm gonna lock the door now, so you got your privacy. But you're ready to go, or you need anything? You just ring that little buzzer over here, and I'll come fix you up. Okay? Have a good time," he said.

A new Yale lock.

There's never anything to steal in a whore's room.

He closed the door behind me. I heard it click.

19

Estrella

It wasn't a bad-sized room. I guessed it had been a son's
or daughter's bedroom. In the corner there was a little
sink and a stack of towels, and on the bed a short brown
girl was sitting in a translucent nightgown, knees
together. As soon as the lock clicked, Estrella pulled her
nightgown over her head, got up, and walked toward me.
She was a little thing with a satiny heart-shaped face and
eyes like black dots, and well upholstered everywhere
you looked. If you ran into her, you'd never bruise yourself on a sharp corner. Halfway to me, she gave each
brown nipple a businesslike twist with thumb and forefinger, to make them look festive for the customer, and
when she reached me, she took the drink from my hand
and set it on a coaster on the dresser. Then she draped
her arms around my neck and turned up her face to kiss
me. No one had told her this was the one thing that
wouldn't be expected of her. Her hair was black and loose
on her shoulders, and there was enough of it that you
could smell it. I admitted to myself that I'd picked her
because I'd thought she was the prettiest. I bent down
and pecked her gently on the forehead, then straight-
ened and stared straight ahead again, thinking hard.
There was a curlicued wrought-iron grille over the
window by her bed, painted white. That made sense,
considering. Probably there'd be one over all the girls'
windows. It didn't surprise Estrella, my not kissing her.
She probably thought I didn't want to kiss a whore on the
mouth. She patted my chest and walked off toward the
sink in the corner, then turned and beckoned me over.
There was no expression at all on her tiny-eyed face, not

even a look of resignation. They hadn't lied much about her age. She couldn't have been more than sixteen, and I could feel it start to build up inside me, the way it does. You heard about places like this, but you always hoped people were exaggerating. They'd come here answering want ads for dancers or domestics, and then the Yale lock would click and somebody, the pimp probably, would sit them down and tell them what they'd be doing with their days from then on. They'd be illegals, mostly, who didn't speak much English. They wouldn't have anyone here to worry about them. They wouldn't be able to yell for a cop. I wondered how old Estrella would be when they let her out. I wondered what she'd be made to do between now and then. I felt my heart grinding inside me now, as if it were being squeezed through a hole too small for it, a hole with sharp edges, and my blood going, and I saw that I'd made my decision. It would make a lot of noise, and probably be kind of tough on the pimp, but none of that could be helped.

When I didn't come over, that didn't surprise Estella either. There'd be lots of men who didn't think they needed to wash. She walked back to me, sank to her knees, and took hold of my belt. I picked her up and set her on her feet again.

"No," I said. "Let me think."

She waited. She had a deep belly button and a round dark belly. I wanted to rest my face against it. I caught myself thinking that twenty minutes wouldn't make any difference. That she probably wouldn't even mind. But that was the point. She ought to have been able to mind. "You don't speak English, do you," I said.

She was silent.

"Put your nightgown on," I said. "Here. Sit down. Here, next to me. Listen. Some bad things are going to happen now. Some, some unpleasant things. But not to you. And when they're done happening, you'll be able to leave. Out." I gestured. *"Afuera. Libre."*

She began to have a look in her eyes, one of fright. She still didn't move.

I took her by the elbow and led her around to the far side of the bed. "Lie down," I said, gesturing. "Down. On the floor, here. And whatever you do, whatever you hear, don't move, don't say anything, until I come for you. I'm going to come for you." She didn't like any of this a bit, but it had been a long time since she'd even thought of trying to stop what she didn't like, and she lay down on the floor. I pulled the spread from the bed and covered her up head to toe. "Okay," I told her. *"Silencio. Siempre silencio."* I went to the door and pressed the buzzer.

I leaned on it a while, and then gave it a few petulant jabs, and by that time I heard heavy footsteps down the hall and the pimp saying, "Easy, easy. I hear you."

"What the hell kind of joint is this?" I shouted querulously through the door.

"Easy, friend. Just give me a minute," he said, putting the key in the lock.

"I want you to see something," I snapped. "I want you to have a look at this." The door opened and the pimp came in. His left hand held a ring of keys and right hand was up near his gun, just in case. He wasn't entirely stupid. I gave him the edge of my forearm across his throat, then opened my hand and yanked him foreward and off balance by the back of the neck, while my left hand slipped in ahead of his right and closed on his gun. It was a big fella, and I held on as he dropped away from it. By the time he hit the floor, I'd switched it to my right hand. He tried to sit up, choking, and I leveled the barrel at his mouth.

"You make a loud noise with that," I said, "and I'll make a loud noise with this."

"Don't shoot me," he whispered raggedly. "Don't shoot me."

I pressed the door closed with my rear.

"Delores has the day's take," he whispered rapidly. "It's just in a pouch. The safe's in the pantry, but I swear to God we don't have the key. I swear to God. They send a guy with the key to transfer the money a couple times a week. Don't shoot me."

"Get down on all fours," I said. "Like that. Good. Does that key open all the rooms?"

"All the girls' rooms."

"Same key for all of them? Show me which. Slowly."

"This one. Don't shoot me, I swear to God."

"Push it closer. How many customers right now?"

"Four. You and three others. In Two, Five, and Six. Two's downstairs."

"Where do you get the girls?" I said.

"What?"

"Where do you get the girls? Ads for singers and cleaning ladies, like that?"

I wanted him to tell me I had it wrong, that this was a plain old cathouse.

"Sure," he said. "Some from bars. I get a commission. Please, guy."

"How often do the girls get to go out?" I said.

"They get supper in the kitchen and a bath down the hall twice a week."

"I mean leave the house."

"Jesus Christ, they don't leave the *house*! Jesus, buddy, don't shoot me."

"What about when they get sick? Or too old?"

He didn't say anything.

I said, "How often does Halliday come by?"

"Who the hell is Holiday?"

"Jesus Christ," I said. "Jesus Christ. Jesus Christ, isn't

this Halliday's joint? Whose is it, Scarpa's?"

"He'll kill me."

"I'll kill you. Is this place Scarpa's?"

"You moron," he said, weeping, "you crazy goddamn moron, everything in this valley is Scarpa's. He'll kill me. He'll kill me."

"No he won't," I said, and shot him.

I put it in his forehead. It was probably cleaner than he deserved. He rocked back and then flopped down on his face and there was a little shriek from under the bed-spread, but then she was still again, like I'd told her. I put another in the back of his head for insurance and then stood there a minute, rubbing my face with my free hand and muttering, "Wrong. Wrong. Wrong." But I'd known it was a dumb play before I pushed the buzzer. I pulled the sheet from the bed and dropped it over the pimp, so Estrella wouldn't have to see him on her way out. I was getting goofier by the minute. "Be right back," I said, and reached over the bed to pat the hump in the bedspread. Then I ran downstairs three steps at a time. There was a lot of hollering behind the locked doors as I went by.

Delores was standing in the middle of the living room, looking wildly up the stairs, clutching a sawed-off shotgun by the barrel and stock. When I appeared, she flung it away with a little yip and ran. I caught her at the door. "Give me your purse," I said. She nodded enthusi-astically and lunged for the door again. I hauled her back. "Purse," I reminded her. She nodded again and lunged the other way, toward the writing table. Her dress bared her back to the coccyx, and all the skinny muscles were twitching like cut worms as she hunkered and snatched up her purse, which had been sitting by a table leg in plain sight. She held it out to me and I tossed it on the sofa.

"The day's take," I said. She yanked open the top

•

drawer of the table and scrabbled inside. The money was in a long canvas wallet with a zipper, the kind bank messengers use. I tossed it next to her purse. I grabbed her by the middle, slung her over my shoulder, and headed out the door as she kicked her legs around above my head. I couldn't tell whether she was trying to kick me or just keep from falling off. Halfway across the road I started fumbling for my car keys. It's hard to do while you're running, especially with a woman on your shoulder. I opened the trunk. "Hey," she said. "Hey listen." I dumped her inside and slammed the lid.

When I got back upstairs it was pandemonium, the doorknobs rattling, a riot of frightened or angry voices behind them. I could stop running now. The doors didn't have to hold much longer. I went back into Estrella's room and said "Time to go," and she threw off the bedspread and sat up, her impassive face slick with tears. I held out my hand. She took it, stepping around the pimp's body without looking down, and we went next door. I put the key in the lock lefty, the way the pimp had, with the gun in my right hand. Inside was a Negro girl wearing just a middy blouse and one pink ankle sock, and a thin handsome man with his shirt buttoned up wrong. He thrust a gold watch and a wad of cash at me, blinking wildly. I took the money and put it in my pocket. "Get going," I said, and he belted past clutching his shoes and jacket. I caught the girl by the arm as she tried to follow and said, "Not yet." She tried to kick me with the foot wearing the sock, and I grabbed her ankle and lifted, then scooped her up in my gun arm as she fell backward. She lay in my arms and gazed up at me as if I'd said a rude word. "Behave," I said, and set her on her feet beside Estrella. I had them join hands, then took Estrella by the hand and led the procession over to the next room. After the first two rooms, Estrella got the idea and started grabbing the women herself as they came out and adding them to the daisy chain. It worked better that way. We finished the four upstairs rooms and then trooped downstairs to do the other three. One other customer offered me his money, and I took it. One had to be dragged from under the bed. Then I threw them both out. I led the girls back into the parlor and surveyed my haul. Seven women of various colors, shapes, and ages, naked or half-naked, standing in a row before me. They were still holding hands, waiting. For a moment I wanted to raise my arms and lead them in a chorus of *Silent Night*. "Okay," I said, "who speaks English?"

"I speak," said one of the Mexicans.

She was olive-skinned, built like a tree stump, and old enough to be most of their mothers. Naked as she was, she stared at me as if she were in a suit of armor. I liked the looks of her. I said, "What's your name?"

She said, "Soledad."

"What are you going to do if I turn you loose?"

"Gonna run."

"What about these girls?"

"Gonna take 'em."

"Where?"

"My cousin farm."

"What'll they do there?"

"Work."

"Where's your cousin's farm?"

"I'm no tell you," she said.

"Good girl," I said. "Have 'em back here, dressed and ready to go, in five minutes. Not six. Five." I held up five fingers.

She nodded, and as I went into the kitchen I heard her snapping a lot of words I didn't understand, and feet thumping up the stairs and down the back hall.

The kitchen door was standing open. Jeeves and his

wife were long gone. The safe was in the pantry, as advertised. It wasn't a safe, but a steel lockbox, which made me feel lucky. Two shots from the pimp's .45 did for the lock, and I pried the mangled lid open with a knife from the silverware drawer, mashing my thumb while I was at it. There was about eleven hundred dollars inside and nearly three hundred in the canvas wallet, plus around a hundred from the customers. I divided the pile roughly seven ways. There was eighteen bucks in Delores's purse. I stuffed it in my pocket, along with her car keys and driver's license, then trotted back to the parlor. The girls were all there, holding pocketbooks or bulging pillowcases, dressed in everything from torch singers' gowns to a suit of men's pajamas, and Soledad was standing in front of them with folded arms. I handed them each their cut and gave the car keys to Soledad. "There are three cars outside," I told her. "A beat-up brown Hudson across the street and two others next to the house. The keys will fit one of the two by the house. Get as far as you can before morning, but don't drive to your cousin's farm, or anywhere near. They can trace the car."

"Yes," she said.

"Buy bus tickets. You've got plenty for that. Don't try selling the car, either. Just park it on a side street with the key in the ignition and walk away."

"I'm no stupi'," she said.

"Good. Go."

She came over, took hold of my shoulders and tugged until I stooped, then rose on tiptoe and pressed her hard lips against my cheek. Then she turned, flicked a stubby hand at the others, and led them out the front door.

Estrella didn't move. She stood there, staring with her black-dot eyes. She wore the hacked-up communion dress again. It didn't fit any better. In her fists she held a silvery beaded purse and the wad of money. She still hadn't opened the purse and put the money in. On her feet she wore heavy leather sandals. "I'll go with you," she said.

Her voice was tiny but clear.

I shook my head.

"I'll go with you," Estrella said again.

I stood there.

Soledad marched back inside and grabbed her arm. *"No con eso, chica,"* she said crisply. *"Eso es un malo."* She gave me a hard, brilliant smile and dragged Estrella stumbling out the door, staring back over her shoulder all the way.

I went over to the window. They were disappearing around the corner of the house.

I opened the window and began working my way through the ground floor, opening windows as I went. If they were stuck, I kicked them in. I heard a car start up and drive off. There was an old tin of silver polish and a small can of kerosene under the sink, a half-full can of gasoline by the back stoop, and a pile of Spanish newspapers in the corner. I used the kerosene and gas to soak down the parlor sofa, drapes, and rug, scattered the newspapers around, and set the tin of silver polish on the coffee table. I opened the front door and fumbled in my pockets for matches. All out. I flicked my cigarette lighter until it caught, tossed it underhand at the sofa, and ran, pulling my jacket up around my face. There was a great *whump*, as if someone had struck me with an enormous scalding pillow, and I felt a few bits of glass strike my back. I kept trotting across the street to my car and opened the trunk. Delores tried to scramble back into the corner behind the spare. "Get up," I said.

"Please," she hissed, weeping. *"Please."*

I hauled her out by the arms, and she staggered and braced herself against the back fender. She'd left a shoe in the trunk. She looked wildly at the burning house behind me, and then at my face. She seemed to be all white eyes, in which the fire danced and shook in little sparks. I took her by the throat and stuck the pimp's gun in her mouth. She closed her lips around it for a moment by instinct, then stood there holding the barrel in her bared teeth.

I said, "When you heard the shots, you started running. You didn't even stop to grab your purse. You've got no idea who it could have been. Nobody came by tonight but the regulars. What did I just say?"

I took the gun from her mouth.

She gasped, "I didn't see nothing."

It was pretty corny stuff, the gun in the mouth, but I couldn't think of anything better and I stuck it back in. There was a noise like a cannon shot behind me—the tin of polish—and she jerked and bit down on the barrel. I guess that hurt her teeth. It would have hurt mine. She began weeping again. There were two sharp cracks as her shotgun went off. I pulled her driver's license from my pocket and held it so she could see her picture and read her name and address. "If anyone comes to see me, I'll come to see you. If they come see me, I'll come see you. What did I just say?" I pulled the gun from her mouth again.

"You'll kill me," she said. "You'll kill me if I talk. You'll kill me."

"Get going," I said, and she kicked off her other shoe and started running barefoot across the field. There was nothing middle-aged about the way she ran. She moved like a high school sprinter.

I watched the fire lighting her twisting white back until it disappeared in the trees. I fished her shoe out of the trunk and threw it after her. I was very tired. Letting her go had been another dumb play. If I could scare her silent, someone else could scare her noisy. If the pimp had earned his bullet, so had she. I pulled out a corner of my shirt and began wiping down his gun, feeling the heat of the fire on my back. I kept staring into the black orchard. Estrella might do all right on a farm someplace. It was probably where she'd come from. I can usually tell another kid from the country. I wasn't a farmer's son, but I grew up in a farm town and I've pulled rye and cut wheat. I thought for a moment of Estrella in a plain decent dress, on her own place somewhere, with a lot of black-haired kids that hopefully didn't look too much like me, and her plump little body next to mine at night. I wouldn't have been the first old slob out there with a young wife who didn't speak much English. Yeah, well. My cousin farm. For all I knew, Soledad would put the girls straight into another house. I hadn't reached Halliday, either. All I'd done was make bad smells and loud noises, and all I had to show was eighteen dollars and a dead pimp. No, I'd left ten bucks in the tray. One of the girls had it now. Eight dollars and a dead pimp. The fire reached the gas line in the kitchen then and made me jump. I tossed the pimp's gun in the ditch and drove back to town. Halfway there I remembered there wasn't anything at home, not even coffee, so I stopped at an all-night diner and bought myself a couple plates of chicken hash with Delores's money.

20
Letter

I expected to feel pretty bad the next day, but as it happened I didn't feel much of anything. When I thought it through again, I still couldn't see a way to turn the girls

loose without killing the pimp. Not without getting
cooled myself, then or later. I don't pretend I know what
people deserve, but the girls couldn't stay there and I figured I had at least as much right to be perpendicular as
the pimp. Actually, I did feel bad, like hell in fact, but
about Metz's tongue. It was Metz I still couldn't stop
thinking about. That didn't make sense to me, but there's
no law that things have to make sense to me, and eventu-
ally I said the hell with it and went out to buy groceries.

I was planning to get juice, bread, bacon, eggs, potatoes, and a pound of coffee. While I was there I figured
I'd better get some spaghetti and maybe some ground
beef, and then I thought I ought to have some vegeta-
bles, growing boy like me, and some fixings if I wanted to
make stew or a casserole, and by the time I was done I'd
spent just about all I had on groceries. I didn't really
regret it. There's worse things to blow your money on. It's
good having a house full of food. When I pulled back into
the lot at home, I noticed a gleaming gull-wing Mercedes
parked in one of the slots. It was empty. No one with any
business at the Harmon Court would be driving a car like
that. I got out carrying one of the bags and put a hand to
the hood. Warm. I set my groceries down on the sidewalk, got my gun from the glove compartment, and
walked around the corner of the manager's office,
holding it down by my leg.

The pool was deserted, as usual, except for the drifting
clots of brown algae that weren't supposed to hurt you. It
was a bright morning and the sun was in my eyes. That
wasn't so good, and I considered swinging around and
coming in the other way, but if they were watching from
my window I didn't want them to notice I'd noticed anything. The gun was down behind my right leg where they
probably couldn't see it. Then the shadow of the Sun-Glo
Girl's elbow fell across my face and I blinked in the dim-

ness. My front door was half open. I strolled up at a little angle so whoever was inside wouldn't have a clean shot, and when I was almost to the door, I kicked it open and spun back against the wall. Nothing. I barged into the room, gun first.

Scarpa had pulled my desk chair to the middle of the rug, and was sitting there reading *The Red Badge of Courage*, one leg crossed neatly over the other. He looked up and said, "You gave me a start, with that bang. This is a pretty good book."

"It's one of my favorites," I said, my gun trained on his pocket handkerchief.

"This is an old book? Famous?"

"That's right."

"It's a pretty good book. You mind I borrow it?"

"Go ahead."

I lowered the gun.

Scarpa lay the book face down on his knee, open to keep his place, and looked around the room. "You live like a pig," he said.

"I thought I kept it pretty neat."

"That's what I mean. Imagine having to keep a place like this neat."

"You're a hard man to please."

"It's not true," he said. "I'm easy to please. All I want is people acting sensible, doing what they say, and I'm pleased. Of course, they got to do what I say, too."

I stuck the gun in my pocket. My hand was sweaty, and I wiped it on my leg.

"I had a little trouble last night," he said. "Somebody came to one of my businesses. Not a big business, just a little business of mine. But they chased everybody away, and shot a guy works for me. And then they burned the place down."

"What, the whorehouse?"

"Oh, you know all about it?"

"It's in the papers. That was your whorehouse? I wouldn't brag about being in that line of work."

"Just a little business," he said, "and it's not enough they got to kill everybody. They got to *burn* it. Right down to the ground. And I'm thinking, who do I know like that? Who do I know's a goddamn Mau-Mau that doesn't know when to stop? I thought I taught you something. I thought you knew how to screw the lid on."

"It's a big town, Lenny. Every now and then something happens I don't do."

"You didn't burn down my whorehouse?"

"I didn't burn down your whorehouse. Why would I?"

"That's what I'm asking."

"I've got no reason to do it. Where's the percentage?"

"No percentage."

"Well then," I said and lifted my palms.

"I'll tell you something," he said. "It's the God's truth. As long as I been doing this, I have never gunned anybody without a reason. It's sloppy. You start gunning people just cause you got guns and everything goes to hell."

"Good. Don't gun me."

"I got a feeling about you, Corson. But a feeling's not a reason."

"No."

"But I'll tell you what I'll do," he said. "In twenty-four hours, no, let's be nice. In seventy-two hours. I want you living someplace else. Some other city. Where I never see you or hear about you again. All right? Someplace far away. I'm not gonna come here again. I'll send people. And Wednesday afternoon, if you're still here? I'll have my reason. Cause you didn't do what I say."

He closed the book and stood. "This was a nice short conversation," he said, and walked to the door.

When he was halfway along the pool, he called back, "Thanks for the book."

In a minute I heard the Mercedes start up, and then it ground off into the distance.

I put my desk chair back where it goes and opened up my trunk to see if he'd mussed my books. Then I opened the closet and sniffed. You could still smell the smoke on my jacket. It was nice Scarpa hadn't thought of that, but I didn't think he'd make enough mistakes to save me.

Aside from the chair, he hadn't disturbed anything, but I walked around fiddling and putting things to rights anyway. My books, my bed, my clothes, my desk. It had been a pretty good room. I'd liked being here. There were plaid curtains, and I'd gotten used to seeing them when I woke up in the morning. They let me know that I wasn't back on the road again. It was the first place I'd ever had a bathroom to myself, and I always kept it so it shone, so no one would ever be able to go in there and say, This is some bum's bathroom. When you've been on the road, you hate to leave a room. You know they might not let you have another.

My bag of groceries was still on the front walk, and I fetched it back and got the rest from the car, and then put them all away in the kitchen. I'd planned a big breakfast and that's what I had: four eggs up, a couple stacks of flapjacks, about half the bacon, a few pieces of buttery rye toast, and coffee. Then I cleared the dishes and washed the pans and drank another cup, slowly, while I read the paper with my feet up on the guest chair. And then I went for a ride, because the car was all mine now, bought and paid for.

I had it in mind to take a spin along the coast, with the waves rolling and racing as if they were skipping along with the car, and the sun warming my face and the clean wind in my hair, but I don't drive a convertible and I wound up in a second-run movie theater on Pascal. It was some kind of science fiction deal. I'd come in in the middle. These octopus-things that lived in craters were dragging the spacemen underground. It was a planet of women, and you could tell their queen was evil because her eyebrows were pointy, and you could tell she was the queen because her collar stuck up in back higher than her head. When she was upset, she did these interpretive dance moves. There was a lot of running through tunnels, and finally the walls were toppling in, the queen dancing around clutching her temples, and then you saw the palace burning, the little minarets toppling off, and a big THE END in the sky. I sat there for a few minutes watching cartoon squirrels whack each other with mallets, and then it started up again. The rocket came down on a column of fire. The men set out across a kind of meadow. Way off on the horizon, the palace appeared, shining and perfect. I got up out of my seat and went to see Rebecca.

The stairs still weren't anything that would interest Busby Berkeley. At the top of them, I heard voices. They got louder as I neared Number 6. It sounded like I wasn't the only one having a bad morning. I paused in front of the door, listening. Down the hall, the manager's door was shut. Inside I heard Shade and Rebecca going at it pretty strong. I was coming at a bad time. Okay by me. The worse, the better. I knocked on the door, and when no one answered, I opened it.

Rebecca wore a pair of beige slacks and a brassiere. Her hair was uncombed and her feet were bare. Shade was dressed just as he'd been the previous Friday, except I couldn't see his hat anywhere. His face was dark and ugly, and his enormous neck seemed to be swelling as I watched. When I came in, he slowly pivoted his entire body to look at me. It was like watching a gun turret turning. "Why, it's Misser Carson," he said.

"Ray," Rebecca said, not looking at me. "Get out of here."

I said, "Hello, Shade. Rebecca."

"Why it's Mister Carson. H'lo, Misser Carson. Nother one a Beggy's frien's. Nice t'know Beggy's so many frien's."

"That's enough now, Lorrie," Rebecca said.

"Real good frien's. Y'wamme t'run along now like a li'l bitty angel and run long now so you c'n talk a Mister Carson?"

"Good idea," I said.

"Shut up, Ray. Lorrie, I want you to calm down now."

"Beggy's poplar gal. Yessir. Nother frien'. Nother frien'. Wamme run long? Be n'angel? No? No? Maybe'll stay then. Stay'n wash. Learn some'n. Yessir, Beggy knows a few th—"

Shade wasn't the only one who could move fast. I saw a white streak, and suddenly Shade's face had snapped to the side and there were three red welts down his cheek.

"Shut up," she whispered. "Shut up. Shut up. Shut up."

He looked at her in horror—I was probably looking at her the same way—and his eyes slowly filled with tears. "I'm sorry, Becky. I didn't mean it."

"Get out of here. Go away."

"I didn't mean it, Becky," he said, beginning to sob. "I didn't mean nothing, Becky."

"You miserable fat-faced lump of hillbilly cowboy feeble-minded—you'll never mean anything. You'll never mean anything. Go *away*."

She began to swear at him then, one hard spurt after another of vile language. She didn't use any words I didn't know, and I guess I wasn't surprised she knew them herself, but it was shocking to hear them in those clear, familiar, almost prissy tones—her diction hadn't coarsened at all—and pouring out through a red distorted face I wouldn't have recognized.

"Don't, Becky," Shade kept saying. "Becky, don't."

He pronounced it *dawn*.

Swearing furiously, she wrangled him through the door and slammed it.

"I'll go crazy," she said to no one special. "I'll go right straight out of my goddamned mind. This is hell. This is *hell*." She looked at me with hatred. "What do you want here with your big fat face?"

Then she went still. Her eyes, which she'd twisted small, grew huge, terrifyingly large, and she spun and yanked the door open again.

Shade was still standing there, weeping. "Becky," he said.

The noise that came from her now wasn't speech at all, just a sound like heavy chain being dragged over rock. She lunged forward at Shade and began driving him down the hall with her fists. I heard them shuffling slowly along the carpet, and her voice echoing. She was expressing herself, all right. He was getting it with the bark still on.

The moment they were out of sight, I went to the little desk. Nothing there or in the closet. The top drawer of the bureau was socks and undies. In the second drawer I found the powder-blue appointment book. I flipped through it. Mostly blank. The first three months were gone. In the back there was a string of phone numbers next to single initials, and I tried to commit the first two to memory. I looked in the pocket in the back cover, from which she'd taken the snapshot of Halliday. Inside was a letter on plain white stationery, with no envelope. It had been folded and refolded so often it was fragile along the creases. I read:

Dear Becky,

   Well Kid it looks like the Movie Star idea is a bust as we thought it might be but I'm not down hearted and I don't want you to be either. I got a number of other things working just at the moment and I think I'm doing O.K. or anyhow I could be if a few things would work out like I'm planning but my spirits are good and this is not as bad a Town as I was thinking. But I wish I had my girl with me. Because then I know everything would really go then. Honey there are more girls here then you could think of a million girls but there aren't any of them like you, like a queen, and I think you should come out here because when they see you here they'll know they really got something. I'm serious when I say that you could go big around here. Baby they think they've seen something but they haven't seen athing till they've seen you. I'd like to see you up there getting treated like you deserve and I wouldn't be a bit suprised to find you got that little something they seem to think I lack, and also I never think so clearly as when your here with me. If we were working this town together nothing could stop us. And even if they did I wouldn't care anyway if you were here. I'm taking a little liberty and enclosing as you can see a ticket on the Western Zephiyr. I wish I was sending you an airplane ticket instead but that'll come in time. Baby just come for a visit to lift my spirits and if you don't like it I'll get you home again someway but I know the way I really know things that this is your kind of Town.

   All my love allways,
   "Lance"

I heard a door slam down the hall, and footsteps approaching. She walked back into the room saying, "I'll kill him. I'll *kill* him."

When she saw me holding the letter, she stopped.

She walked over to the straight chair by the closet. She sat herself down cautiously, as if she wasn't sure the chair would hold.

We looked at each other.

"You met him a few months ago when he hired you to do a stag movie," I said.

She didn't say anything.

I said, "So you did a couple movies and then stole his money, because he wasn't much of anything to you anyway, and now he wants to douse you with lye."

"May I have that, please," she whispered.

"Sure," I said, and handed her the letter.

"May I have my book, please."

I gave that to her, too, and she folded the letter carefully and tucked it away where it had been and zipped up the book.

She gripped the book in both hands.

"I know," she said. "I know I've lied to you. But I haven't lied about anything important, Ray. Not important to you. Only to me."

"Uh huh."

"If you're going to hit me," she said, "then go on and hit me, but please don't just keep standing over me like this."

I sat down on the bed.

"Thank you," she said.

"Take it from 'important,' " I said.

"Please," she said.

"Becky," I said. "Tell me what's going on."

"I didn't lie, really," she said. "Everything important was true. From your end. I do need to get away from him. He did say he'd burn my face. The only thing different is that I didn't just meet him because he wanted girls for his movies. The only thing is that I've known him, that we grew up together, in the same little town. And I loved him very much. And there was only him, and he loved me too. If you read the letter—back then he loved me too. He wrote such wonderful letters, and he was going to send for me, and he did send for me. And when I got here I couldn't understand anything, because back home everyone liked us, and wished us well, because we were such nice kids. We were. We were athletes and we were nice kids. And for a while, when I was here, I thought everything he was doing must be all right, because it was him doing it. And then I thought, if the other things, if he wasn't right according to those things, then I'd have to get rid of everything else that said he was wrong. Because I loved him. And I made movies for him. And I did other things. And I began turning, I've turned into something horrible. I had to get away. I have to get away. Because I don't even have his love anymore. But he can't stand to lose anything, even if he has all the others, and he said he'd ruin me if I went, and then I took some money to make a new start with, and that made it worse. Ray?" she said, tears trickling down her face. "Didn't you ever have something so precious, what a stupid word. Something that seemed to justify the whole world, and it went ugly, so ugly. And afterward, you wanted to pretend it had never been. That you'd never been that wrong, or hurt that badly."

"No," I said. "I haven't."

"I did," she said. "And I thought I was so lucky. And I still don't know how it happened. And I don't even believe it's him anymore. You're so surprised I want him hurt, but it doesn't matter, because he's already dead. He must be, dead for years, and now it's somebody else, someone horrible. Because in high school he was so lovely and there was only each other."

"And what high school was this?"

"Do you really need to know that, too?"

"Jesus *Christ*," I roared, and lurched to my feet. She shrank back against the wall.

"Too many goddamned stories," I said, almost choking. "Too many goddamned people telling me too many goddamned things. Something so precious—you don't know what you're doing. I don't know what you're doing. Here." I was digging money from my pocket. There was almost nothing left. I threw it all on the bed. "Here Here's what's left. It's what I've got left. For fifteen bucks a day I'm anybody's chump, but not yours anymore. Not yours. Get yourself another. I'm out. I'm out." I turned and headed for the door.

"Where are you *going*?" she wailed.

"I'm out," I said, and wrenched open the door.

"You can't go," she said, and was across the room and her arms were around me. She clutched at my shoulder and somehow got me facing her again, and got herself plastered against me like a windblown scarf, and got the door closed. We stumbled back against it. "Don't go," she said. "You can't go." Her voice was flat with terror. I couldn't see her face. She was rubbing it, open-mouthed, against my neck, and hauling my shirttails out of my pants and scraping at the small of my back with her fingers. "You can't go," she hissed. "You can't. You can't. Don't go." She was rubbing the whole front of herself against me from chin to knees, back and forth, as if my name were written in chalk on a wall and she needed to rub it out, and I smelled again the scent of harsh white soap, the kind you wash the laundry with, not your own body.

Over her shoulder, I was counting the money on the bed. "It doesn't figure," I said thickly. "If a buck gets me one of them, and twenty-one bucks gets me two, are you telling me twenty-six dollars and forty cents buys the whole package?"

"Don't go," she said.

I shut up.

21
Difference

I never told Mattie what it was like. I wouldn't have known how, anyway. Rebecca knew an awful lot, and she did an awful lot, and for a while I thought I must be a hell of a fellow. Then I saw that the noises she made and the things she said and did were just that, things she said and did. And then I saw they weren't even meant to fool me. She was just trying to show me a good time. I stopped.

"What," she said.

I didn't say anything. I couldn't see her face in the shadows.

"I warned you," she said softly.

"No. What you said was you weren't very good."

"I meant that I don't want anything. I never want anything. It's okay," she said, touching my face. "Don't stop. It's okay."

"Was it—"

"It's never been any different with anybody. But I was happy when it was him. It's okay. Don't stop. Come here. It's okay."

What got to me most, I think, was that I couldn't do anything to get her nipples up. They were just pale disks, sometimes a little nubbly. Of course, some women are like that, even if they're having a fine time. Anyway, it was stupid to take it personally.

Shade tapped on the door once near midnight, softly calling Becky's name, and once a few hours later. The first time Rebecca screamed at him to go away, and the second time she just made the noises she was already making, but a little louder. I heard him weeping and stumbling heavily away down the hall.

His hat was on the floor near the window, behind the bed. That's why I hadn't seen it earlier.

When I woke at dawn, Rebecca was on the other side of the bed and facing away from me, curled up in a *C*, all shoulder blades and lion-colored hair. Every now and again she let out a delicate little snore. They were lovely sounds. She didn't smell like soap now. She smelled like bed. I had forty-eight hours left now until Scarpa sent his men, but it's funny how lying with a woman makes you feel safe for a little while anyway. Still, forty-eight hours isn't much, no matter how good Rebecca smelled, and I got up carefully, knelt down on the floor, and started going through her clothes. There was some pale light coming in under the blinds, and I held up each label and read it. They were just labels. I don't know anything about women's clothes. I didn't think I could do her closet or dresser without waking her, so I got her purse off the night table, gripped the clasp in my fist to muffle the click, and slowly twisted it open. Her purse was nice and tidy. She had a clean lace handkerchief in there, a change purse with about a dollar in change, six singles held together with a paper clip, two shades of lipstick, and a compact I didn't open. There was no driver's license. There was a little chrome .32 automatic with a fake pearl grip. I could have hidden the whole thing in my hand. I broke it and sniffed, looked down the barrel, then popped out the magazine and counted six bullets. Full, and hadn't been fired in a long while. I slid the magazine back in. It went home with a faint click, and I heard

Rebecca stop mid-snore. She was watching me from her nest of fair hair. "Don't you ever stop," she said, without love.

"Morning," I said.

"Morning. If you wanted to see what was in my purse, why didn't you ask?"

"I'm shy."

"I've given you this," she said, patting the sheet over her middle. "I've given you all this. You think I wouldn't've given you what's in my purse? Go on. Take it."

"I'd look pretty silly with a gun like this," I said. "I've never understood why anybody would put chrome on a gun." I pulled out a corner of the sheet and began wiping it down.

"What're you doing?"

"Someday, when you do something stupid with this, I don't want them to find any of my prints on it."

"I thought I'd better get one," she said. "You're probably going to tell me I got the wrong kind."

I examined the gun on both sides in the light from under the blinds, holding it by the sheet, then dropped it back into her purse and set her purse back on the night table. I flopped down beside her. She lay on her back with the blanket drawn up to her chin, the edge of it bunched loosely in her fists, but when I took hold of it myself she let go at once, and I slowly drew it down to the foot of the bed. I propped myself on one elbow and just looked. There wasn't an inch of her that was unfamiliar now. In one way I felt as if we'd been lying around naked all our lives, but in another way I felt I'd just stolen my first peek at her through some bathroom window, as if I was some lucky dirty lad alone in an alley. She lay there gazing at the ceiling, arms at her sides.

"You could say something nice," she said bleakly. "You could tell me I'm beautiful."

"You look ridiculous," I said. "You look like two balloons on a string."

"Thank you. I know. And *you*," she went on savagely, "look *awful*. You did look stupid with my gun. You looked like some big horrible stupid hairy animal. And so *pleased* with yourself. You don't look a bit like a bear. Bears look nice."

"Nice? We had some bears where I'm from. Browns and a few grizzlies. They say people are the only animals that kill for fun. It's not true. A grizzly will do it just to pass the time."

"I know about bears but they still look nice. They have little eyes, and they always look like they're looking around, trying to figure things out."

"Well, that's me in a nutshell. How did we got onto bears?"

"I don't know. It was something I thought of."

We lay there a while in silence. Her breasts and thighs were beginning to goose-pimple, but she didn't try to pull up the blanket. There was a hard flat spot in the center of her chest, and I touched it with a forefinger, then traced my finger down her narrow belly. I picked up one of her legs by the calf, gave it a little shake, let it drop. Her legs didn't touch except at the knee, the way some skinny women's don't, but also, her shoulders were wide enough that her arms didn't touch her sides. There was a clean pale hollow under her arm, and I stroked it with my thumb. She wasn't ticklish. Her muscles were long, flat, and delicate, and braided together like the muscles in a doe's flank. Most pretty women look better with their clothes on, but you had to see all of that goofy body for it to make sense.

"Yes you're beautiful," I said, defeated. "Of course you're beautiful. Why the hell do beautiful women need to keep hearing it?"

She snickered.

"Why do de dames need to hear it?" she growled. *"Why do dey put chrome on de gun?"*

"You like 'em big and dumb, like me and Shade?"

"I don't like 'em any way at all," she said seriously. "When we get the money and I can feel safe again, I'm going to get out of here and go someplace no one's ever heard of me, and get a nice house, with everything nice, and live like a lady. And never have anyone bothering me again."

"What money was that?"

She rolled up on one elbow, and now we were face to face. "We're going to kill him," she said. "We're going to kill him and take his money. It's the only way. He's not going to stop otherwise. He's not ever going to stop. Ray, the smut's old stuff. Halliday's been selling drugs for almost a year. He's been selling cocaine, and you can't imagine the money. Ray, sometimes there's half a million dollars in his safe. We'll split it sixty-forty. That's two hundred grand for you."

"Where do you get sixty-forty?"

"It's my idea and my information. You're just along for the strong-arm work."

"I'd be taking all the risk for my forty. Someone catches me in the house, you never heard of me."

"I'll be there with you," she said. "You think I'm going to tell you how to do it and where the money is, and when, and then have you do the job alone and take off? We'll be there together. You'll make him open the safe. He can't bear pain. We split the money right there. We leave by separate doors and never see each other again."

"I don't mind the money a bit, but it's fifty-fifty. And let's think whether we can't get it without killing. I told you, murder's not easy. There might be a way that makes a little less mess."

"All right, fifty-fifty, but there's no other way. You have to kill him. You have to. What's the matter, haven't you ever killed anyone?"

"I try not to make a habit of it."

"You've got to do it. It's the only way. It's the only way he'll ever leave me alone. You don't know what it's like, when anyone can get at you and do anything. No, that's stupid, of course you do, of course you know. But you're tough, and you can take it, and you know how to do things. I don't know how to do anything. I can't even swim that well anymore. If it wasn't for how I look, I'd make people sick. I make them sick now, but they still have to have me. But when my looks are gone no one will even talk to me. I'm twenty-eight, Ray. They're already half-gone. I was beautiful in high school, I had some meat on my bones. But now I'm just two balloons on a string, and in ten years I'll be two empty balloons on a string, and I have to have money then, I have to have a little money and a place, where people can't get at me, and I can live. I won't ever be married, Ray, you know why. And he's taken so much from me. And now he wants to take my face. I can't be someone no one can stand to look at, and maybe blind, sitting in a room where they bring me a tray and set it down without looking at me. Ray, I need that money. I need him dead. You've got to do it."

"No," I said. "I don't."

She was silent. Then she leaned forward and rested her face against my chest. "Nothing," she mumbled, her mouth half-mashed against me, "nothing I ever do turns out any good."

I kissed her hair and let my mouth rest there. We lay that way a moment, resting.

"Will you at least think about it?" she said.

"Yes."

"Think about it seriously?"

"What do you think I've been doing? Yes."

She lifted her head. "Well. That's an honest answer. You'll think about it. And we'll talk about it later. And you'll make him leave me alone, and get me his money, one way or the other?"

"Yes."

"And we'll split it fifty-fifty. And we'll do it soon, whatever we do. And from now until then, you can have me any time it doesn't interfere, all day if you want, and do whatever you like to me."

"Nice of you."

"No, it's not nice. It's intelligent. I don't want you wandering off again. What, you're not falling in love with me, are you?"

"Probably. You planning to lose much sleep over it?"

She lay back against the pillow and sighed as if she'd just had a big meal. "You're not in love with me. You're not that dumb. You still think I'm beautiful? For now?"

"Yes."

"Not ridiculous?"

"Both."

"You can call me ridiculous. You can call me anything. Come on," she said. "It's too early to get up yet." I pulled the blanket up over her, but she kicked it away. "C'mon," she said. She rolled over on her belly and worked her bony behind up in the air, and waggled it at me like a cop showing a dark gold badge.

I slapped her rump lightly and said, "Put it away. I'm done with it."

She wriggled onto her back again. She smiled and had herself a good stretch. "Mmn. C'mon, slugger. Maybe you can find something I won't do."

"What fun would that be?"

"The fun," she said with slitted eyes, "would be in

making me do it anyhow." She lifted one leg straight up in the air and pointed her toes at the ceiling, then brought her foot slowly around and patted my cheek with it. "When we met," she murmured, "you were going to kick me in the face." She gave my chin a little shove with her toes.

"We hadn't been properly introduced," I said.

"In the *face*," she said, and slapped my cheek lightly with her foot. She gave me a little jab with her toes. "You were gonna kick me in the face. In the *face*," she said, jabbing my ribs with the other foot.

"Hey," I said, and "Ow," but she kept jabbing and slapping with her feet, leaning back on both elbows now with a hard delighted grin and both legs in the air, working, and the whole shooting match wobbling and rolling as I tried to guard my face and gut, until finally I rolled on top of her, and all the play went out of her and she went to work. She locked her knees against my ribs and began to move.

"You think I don't know what you're doing?" I said between my teeth.

Between her teeth she said, "You think you knowing makes any difference?"

22
Dead

When I woke up next, she was gone. I didn't think more than a couple hours had passed. It was almost eight by the alarm clock on her *night* table. I found my watch and checked it. Almost eight. Well, now we'd established that it was almost eight. We were making progress. I put on

my watch, sat on the side of her bed, and tried to think
what I could do to earn my pay. There wasn't a damn
thing I could think of. I was tired of shaking trees with no
fruit on them. I didn't have a lever and I wasn't getting
any closer to one. What I had was Rebecca, and whatever
she knew and hadn't quit dancing around long enough to
tell me yet, and she'd gone missing. Meanwhile, if I had
to leave town tomorrow, or even move across it, I didn't
have much of a stake. I got out my wallet and counted,
thinking about that dinner at Annie Jay's. It was stupid,
spending that kind of money. I'm an eater. It's as bad as
drinking sometimes. I put on my clothes and went down
the sticky stairs. I didn't run into Shade. I found where
I'd left my car and headed over to the hiring hall on
Welliver, even if it was eight-twenty already.

It was past nine when I got there. "Jesus," Bergdahl
said, from behind his old desk. "Look what's here at
lunchtime and wants work."

"Hello, Bergdahl."

"Hello, Ray. What are you doing here? It's practically
noon. I could've used you at seven."

"I overslept."

"Company?" he said, leering.

"I don't know how I got this reputation."

"Company, huh. Well, you got to tend to business if
you want the business."

"I know it."

"We got a lot of early worms here."

"I know it. I just thought I'd come by anyhow."

"Ah, it's slow. I didn't have much this morning either."

"I'm sorry to hear that. I was hoping to pick up something."

"Well, come back Wednesday or so. I been hearing
some things. I think by mid-week, Thursday the latest I
can fix you up."

"Sooner would be better. I don't mind what it is. I'll wheel concrete, if that's what you've got."

"Aw, you that stony?"

"I was hoping I could make a few dollars today."

"Aw, hell. I wish I had something."

"Well, don't fret about it," I said.

He got very interested in his desk blotter then. "I guess you got stuck on those Olindas roofs for Nestor," he said.

"Yep."

"Everybody did. That little spic stuck everyone. I'm sorry, Ray. I'm sorrier than hell. I should've known better."

"We all know what he's like, Bergdahl. I took the work. Don't worry about it."

"I just don't like seeing my guys stuck. That's the last time that rotten little spic hires out of this hall, and I told him so."

"Don't worry about it."

"I've got nothing against a man just cause he's a Mex, you know that. But I have no time for that rotten little spic. Well, I guess I'm not the only one's tired of him."

"What do you mean?"

"You didn't hear? You'll like this story. Three big smokes broke into his office the other day and choked him with a chain until he opened his safe. They got away with two grand. He's been going around showing everybody the marks on his neck."

"Is that a fact."

"Like it?"

"And that little beauty telling us all he was broke."

"I thought you'd like that story."

"The only way I could like it better is if I did it myself and had the two grand."

"I wouldn't put it past you," he said, with a laugh that

didn't quite jell.

"Now what sort of talk is that?" I said.

"Oh, I don't mean anything. But I've seen you get hot, Ray. I just wouldn't put it past you."

"My buddy."

"In fact," he said, sort of unwillingly, "first time heard, I thought of you."

"That's right, Bergdahl," I said. "It was really me. I'm three big shades, and I've got two grand in my pocket, and that's why I'm here begging for unskilled work."

"All right," he said. "Don't listen to me. I'm just giving you the needle."

But he was having trouble meeting my eyes again.

I left soon after.

At home I had a shower and treated myself to a shave and a grilled cheese sandwich. Then I thought what the hell and called Mattie.

"How's Lenny," he said.

"In the pink," I said. "Got anything for me?"

"James Lee Marron, born June 10, 1926. Six two, one ninety-five, blonde and brown. Former star running back of the Porter Eagles."

"That's Halliday?"

"That's Halliday. Former president of the Porter Thespians Club. Scrapes with girls. Scrapes with cops, just kid stuff. Always talked his way out, except for the one time. Left Michigan ahead of a Mann rap in '46. Family hasn't heard from him since '48. Any good to you?"

"Not that I know of, Mattie. But thanks. I appreciate the trouble."

"You don't sound so hot. You don't sound like the gangster bit agrees with you."

"I'm all right."

"Why don't you quit 'em, Ray? Why don't you quit 'em

both before they suck you down and get you where you can't? Come by and talk. There's other things for a guy like you to do than this."

"You've always been a friend, Mattie."

"All right, I'll mind my business. Well, that's Halliday."

"I appreciate it."

"You want his family?"

"Sure," I said. "Yeah, sure. Give me the family."

He gave me the family.

After I hung up the phone, I sat there awhile at the desk, not doing anything at all. Then I thought I'd try a little finger-drumming. Then I drummed my forefingers lightly on the space bar of my typewriter, like playing the bongos. Then I decided to really make a party of it and rolled some paper in.

On the first sheet I typed out *Leave Town*, and then underneath, *W/ what $?* I started typing out a list of what I could pawn or sell. The car. The new clothes. My watch. My books. Not my books. My typewriter. What else? The typewriter wouldn't bring much. Too old. Neither would the suit. Too big. I x'd them both out. It was a cheap watch, which left the car, and without the car, how was I going to travel? Catch a freight again? Hitchhike? Just go back on the bum, like that, after nine years? I pulled out the page and crumpled it up.

I rolled in a new page and wrote *Move Across Town*. L.A. was a big place. Scarpa wouldn't waste time looking for me. Hell, I could go stay with Joanie in Baldwin Park. Sure. Her and me and Lewis. Of course, Hollywood, Culver City—every reason I had for being in this town was on the West Side. Right in the middle of Scarpa's patch. So if I wanted to, I could go crawl into a corner somewhere and live the way Rebecca did, looking over my shoulder every time I left my room. And again, what money was I going to use until I got set up? Sure, sell the

car. And how was I going to get around? Or get to my
new job, once I got it? I pulled out the paper and crumpled it, then smoothed it out, then crumpled it again and
threw it away.

I rolled in a new page and wrote *Talk to Scarpa*. No.
There wasn't a damn thing I could say to Scarpa, nothing
I could offer him. I could show him newsreel footage of
somebody else burning down his whorehouse and he'd
want me gone or dead just the same. He was tired of
thinking about me.

I x'd out *Scarpa* and wrote in *Burri*. But that wasn't
any good either. Burri got a kick out of me, but I'd shut
down one of his lieutenants' businesses. One of his businesses. Could I convince him I hadn't? And even if I
could, the old man might like to ride Scarpa a little, but
he wasn't going to bang heads with him over some yegg
he'd just met.

I wondered what Round Head and Green Eyes were
doing just then. I could see them coming up my walk.
Going to see the cutie, one last time.

I thought about making another grilled cheese sandwich.

I rolled in a fresh sheet and wrote *Exterior. Day*.

I started with a medium shot of a young woman swimming. She was swimming beautifully, and you got the
light moving on the water after she went by, but that's not
a shot to open on, and I x'd it out and tried a long exterior
of a convertible coming down a dirt road. There were
half-built houses all around. A woman behind the wheel.
A little dust coming up behind the car and hanging in the
air. Her hair was loose, but that was all you could tell. You
couldn't see her face, so you kept watching. Her face
could wait. You knew she was beautiful. That was all right
as far as it went, that would photograph, but what then?
She was in trouble, she was on the run. In a car like that?

Sure. Maybe. She was going to meet somebody. She had high hopes and the world on a string, but he was going to set her up, he was going to betray her. He? I felt the air coming out of it. There had to be a guy, but what sort, for a woman like that? I thought of a few and set them talking to her. But she only looked their way because it was in the script, and all that came out of anyone's mouth was Noël Coward crap. I couldn't get them going. All I really had was her moving beautifully and silently, in the water or a blue convertible, no one getting anywhere near. I'd never seen a movie like that, and I didn't think I'd buy a ticket if they made one. I killed a few more sheets, then lay my arms on the desk and my head on my arms. When I opened my eyes it was dark, and someone was hammering on my door and weeping.

I opened the door and Rebecca half-fell inside. "You wouldn't open up!" she shrieked. "You just sat there!"

Her nose had bled down her chin and neck, long enough ago that the blood was drying and her nose was running mucus now over the blood. There was a scrape on her forehead and her hair and dress were filthy with dry red dirt and something that could have been oil. It was a party dress with a satin yoke collar, and it had been ripped down one side so that she had to hold it up with her hand, and the bottom hem was ragged and dangling. One knee had been bleeding and was bleeding again. Her feet were bare and dusty and her stockings hung in dark shreds from her ankles. Her red eyes kept squinting and widening. "You just sat there! I saw you through the window! I *saw* you. Lorrie's dead," she cried, "he's dead, he's the only one who didn't think I was a liar, and now he's dead, and he'll kill me, he'll kill me next."

I held her. Her back was damp with cold sweat. I took her purse and dropped it on a chair. She let go of her dress. It slid down her ribs, and a sharp stink of hysteria rose from inside. "Where's Halliday now?" I said, stroking her cold back.

"I don't care, I don't care," she said, sobbing. "He can kill me if he wants. But I just can't be running *around* like this anymore."

"Becky, does Halliday know you're here?"

"Nobody knows," she sobbed. "Nobody knows."

"Becky. If Halliday's coming, I have to get ready."

"I told you he doesn't *know*. He *left* me out there. He *left* me. Lorrie tried to save me, and he killed him, just shot him, and I thought he was going to kill me too, but he just—" Her voice had risen to something that was almost a whistle, and she had to force the words out. "He took my—*car*! And he was *beating* me! And I was running, and he was *laughing* at me!"

"All right," I told her. "It's all right now."

"He killed him, Ray, he shot him like it was *nothing*. Like it was *nothing*."

"It's okay."

"He'll come here," she said.

"No he won't. You said he doesn't know where you are. Look. I'm locking the door now, and bolting it. That's the only door. And I'm closing the curtains, all right? And look, Becky." I opened the desk and took out my gun. It made a good clunk when I set it down on the blotter. "See? We're ready for anyone. Now let's get you cleaned up a little."

"I'm very dirty," she said.

"You're a sight," I said. I slipped off what was left of her dress and stockings and dropped them in the wastebasket. I undid her brassiere, then gave her a quick once-over and had her move her arms and fingers. Nothing broken. I wrapped her in a blanket and sat her down in the armchair while I ran a bath, and had her watch my fingertip as I moved it around in circles in front of her face. No concussion I could see. The bath was ready then, and I helped her into it. She blinked and looked around, and worked her feet in the water. I handed her the soap and she began to wash the blood from her face.

An Avianca stew had left half a bottle of blue dolls in my medicine cabinet. She only used to need two to put her away for the night. I gave Rebecca four with a finger of Old Overholt. "I don't want it," she said.

"Drink."

I took the glass from her and helped her lather up her hair. "Becky? Where did all this happen?"

"Don't want to think about it."

"Tell me."

"Down past Crenshaw."

"Where exactly?"

"Where Crenshaw jogs over, past 405? As if you're going to the airport, and there's a little hill and those jointed oil things. That look like bugs. Crickets."

"Which one? Near which of the pumps? Can you remember?"

"Don't know. Three or four of them. There's a little silver shack. Listen, Ray?" She sat up in the water and looked at me with wide eyes to show me how reasonable she was being. "I decided, he can have my face if he wants, because don't you think he'd leave me alone then? And be satisfied? It doesn't matter what I look like if he'll just leave me alone, but I can't be running around like this. I can't be scared all the time."

"Close your eyes," I said, and dunked her head in the water. She reached back and worked her fingers through her hair, then sat up again.

"We didn't get it all out," she said. "But don't you think he'd leave me alone then? It doesn't matter what I look like. How I look's never brought me anything good."

"What were you doing down there past Crenshaw?"

"We went for a ride. He must've followed us."

"From where? Where had you been?"

"Don't know."

"We need to dunk you again," I said. "There. I think that's all of it." I lifted one of her feet from the water. "You've got some blisters coming up. Want me to take care of them?"

"Yes please," she said, speaking very clearly. She was starting to go.

I didn't have a needle, so I got out a fresh razor blade and used the corner. She acted as if I was doing it to someone else's feet. "There. Let's get you dried off and in bed now."

I pretty much had to lift her out, and she leaned against me as I toweled her off. "Are you going out there," she murmured.

"Yes."

"Oh." She was silent a while, letting herself be rubbed dry. "Can I have my comb?"

"Sure."

I sat her on the toilet lid and spread some antiseptic salve on her feet and her scrapes, then buttoned her into one of my old flannel shirts and tucked her up in my bed.

"You'll make me . . . " she murmured.

"What?"

She was almost out.

"You'll make me say things," she said.

"No," I said. "I won't."

She went to sleep.

I changed into dry clothes, got my toolbox from the closet and put my gun in my pocket. I turned out the light and left, locking the door behind me.

I cut over to Crenshaw and headed due south. It was the same route she'd driven me last Friday, in the sunshine. The night was coolish, and I opened the window and let the breeze clear the bathroom steam out of my head. It was around six miles to the oil fields, a pretty solid walk for someone in bare feet. Maybe she'd had her shoes on for part of the way. She probably had, and thrown them away when a heel broke. Her feet had looked fairly bad. You can do all sorts of things when you're in shock. Some of the houses and shops I passed were all right, and some weren't so good, and in some places any white woman on foot would have stood out, even if she wasn't bleeding and in rags. But whoever saw her had kept their distance. There are people who seem in such trouble that, whether you're a Samaritan or a hyena, you want to back off, shield your face, as if they were on fire.

As the 405 underpass came up, I could see through it to the big silver curves of the Mobil tanks in the distance. When I got to the other side the road jogged to the right, just as she'd said, and I saw a convertible with its lights on, standing fifteen yards or so from the road. Beside it was a corrugated steel shed with no windows, and behind that, three walking-beam pumps loomed up against the night sky. Rebecca was right. They looked like insects, enormous mantises, bowing and rising very slowly over something on the dark ground I couldn't see. I stopped ten feet from the convertible and killed the lights, but left the motor running. I got out with my gun in my right hand and my flashlight in my left. I didn't turn on the flash. The Studebaker's motor was still running. I didn't see anyone around. Each pump clanked softly at the bottom of each slow stroke. My nostrils were thick with the rank, gluey smell of crude oil.

There was no one in the convertible, dead or alive. No stains on the white vinyl seats. I switched on the flash and walked once around the car, hearing that big V-8 Stude engine purr, looking at the footprints all around. They didn't tell me anything. I followed the scuffed-up dirt around the back of the shed and found Lorin Shade where I thought he'd be. He was on his back, just out of sight of the road, and his pearl-snapped shirt was a black mess underneath his heart.

I put the flash on the mess and thought I could count four holes. I swallowed hard and brought my nose down close to the wounds. There was the smell of blood, half new copper penny, half raw beef, and a smell of scorched cloth. I put the light on Shade's face. He didn't have any opinion of what had gone on. There was thick red dust on his shirt and his face, even on his open eyes. I stood up and thought a while as the pumps went up and down. I walked in a circle around him and the shed, and kept widening the circle a bit with every revolution, my flash on the ground. Maybe fifteen, eighteen feet from Shade's body I found a scrap of lacy cloth, stained gray in the middle. I sniffed it, and then dropped it back on the ground. I wasn't about to introduce it in court. I went to my car, got some surgical gloves from my toolkit, and came back and got into the Stude.

It was the same car, all right, only now I was in the driver's seat. I had a quick, screwy impulse to put it in gear and cruise around a while. I've never driven a car that nice. I opened the glove compartment, but the registration was already gone. There was nothing else in there I needed to think about. Nothing on the floor or under the seats. I killed the lights, turned the engine off, and got out. Someone had thought to take the license plates, too, front and back. Nothing in the trunk, not a thing. It was still the cleanest damn trunk you could imagine, like no one had ever opened it. I closed it, pulled a handkerchief from my pocket, and polished the trunk latch. I polished the gas tank lid too, and all the door handles, and then I got back in and did the steering wheel and gearshift and so on. That was probably everything. I stood there, thinking. The hell, I was tired. I got back in my car and went home.

I spent the night in the armchair, under my overcoat, with my feet propped up on the bed. I woke up at dawn, a little before Rebecca. She hadn't moved. She was thin enough that you could barely see her body under the blankets. All you saw was thick pale hair on the pillow and a face that seemed a little childish in sleep, with the top front teeth showing, which made her look a little rabbity. When she started waking up, I could tell she didn't want to. She knew she was going to remember something bad. It was her turn to wake up that way. She blinked at the ceiling, and then she blinked at me, and then she looked at me.

I said, "All right. I'll take care of him for you."

23
Bed

She took a long time to focus on my face. She had a strand of hair stuck in the corner of her mouth, and she brushed it away. It took two tries. "You were there all nigh'? In the chair?"

"Sure."

"You should'n' be there," she murmured. "You nee' your sleep."

"I slept fine. I've slept worse places than a comfortable chair in a clean room."

"You slept all right?"

"I slept fine."

"You'll take care of him for me?"

"Yeah."

"You need your sleep," she said. "You should sleep in your own bed. Come on. Get into bed. You need your sleep."

There was a stirring under the blankets, and then my shirt dropped out the side of the bed.

"You need to *rest*," she said.

I got up and went around the other side of the bed. I took off my belt so the buckle wouldn't jab her and got in.

"No," she said. "Your skin. Want your arms and your skin."

I got up again, shucked off my clothes, and got back in. She hitched backwards into me bottom-first and pulled my arms around her as if she were getting into a mink coat. "How's the nose?" I said.

"I hurt it," she said. "But it's better." She put my right hand on her left breast and my left hand on her belly. "G'night," she said.

We lay like that for a minute. Then she squirmed around until she was facing me, slung a leg over mine, and gave my collarbone a vague kiss.

"Okay. Good night," she said. "I keep seeing Lorrie."

"It'll be better," I said. "Good night."

"You saw him?"

"Yes. I went and saw him."

"Oh. G'night."

We lay there for a few minutes. Her breath was humid against my throat, and a little sour. "Mmn," she said. "I keep seeing Lorrie. Can you, can I have a little . . . "

She kept tugging at my shoulder and hip until she'd rolled me over on top of her.

"Easy," I said.

"Now," she said. "Now he can't get at me."

"All right. Are you all right?"

"He can't get me now," she said, and wound her legs

around mine. "Can you sleep like this?"

"On top of you?"

"It's safer this way. I'm safe now." She moved sleepily beneath me, getting comfy. I found I was ready again. "Do you want to do some more?" she said, noticing.

"I don't think you're in any shape."

"You have to take care of me now," she said, moving beneath me.

Neither of us put on a stitch of clothing until we left the room that night. Of course, she didn't have any clothing to put on, but she didn't let me get dressed, either. It was different from the first night. She didn't make those nice noises now or say any of those picturesque things, or much of anything at all except *faster* or *easy* or *wait*, and the only sound she made was harsh steady breathing, which choked off every now and then as she thought we might be getting somewhere. I tried to be careful of her bruises, but she didn't want me to be careful. She wanted me to work. She almost didn't care what I did, but she wanted me doing something to her all the time, and she'd clench her teeth like a small animal caught in a trap each time she thought there was some hope. And then little by little she'd see it was no good again and ease off, her face gray and exhausted and the tips of her breasts just pale flat circles.

In between, she sat naked at my desk like a schoolgirl doing lessons and drew Halliday's house from memory on typing paper. She knew it pretty well. She scratched in every stick of furniture and put hash marks through the walls to show where the windows were. She told me how many steps there were in the back stoop and the front stoop, and made a guess about how many there were in the hall stairs.

"Where's the safe?" I said.

She said, "When you've got your money, you can find a

sweet young girl who doesn't mind questions questions questions every minute of the goddamned day."

She made me close my eyes and describe each room from memory as if I were walking through it from the back to the front, and then from the front door to the back, and when she felt I'd gotten it right she took me to bed and rewarded me. But she kept forgetting it was supposed to be my reward and started grinding again.

She was pale everywhere the sun didn't go, and the bruises made her look paler. She looked fragile. I thought of Scarpa and his men, and what they did for a living, and how people are so damn easy to hurt.

For breakfast I made her a big omelette with tomatoes and cheddar, and for lunch I made a tuna casserole with canned salmon instead of tuna, which worked all right, and that night we had a big spaghetti dinner. I'd never been so proud to have a house full of food. People had done it for me sometimes when I was on the bum, but I'd never done it for anyone else, taken them into my house and fed them. When I was cooking, she'd either lean with her cheek against my back, humming, or sit over her plans, noodling and frowning. After lunch, she helped with the dishes, and then we sat side by side on the bed and watched TV, still in the altogether but not mauling each other particularly, as if we were an old married couple. We watched *Friendship Ranch* and part of *Carter and Sharp on the High Seas*. She hooked her leg over mine at one point and took it back when she got pins and needles.

By mid-afternoon the bed was so rotten with sweat that I had Rebecca get up so I could put on fresh sheets. She slumped in my armchair, her knees gangling out, watching me. "You're really making that bed," she remarked.

"It doesn't take any longer to do it right."

"The Army teach you to make a bed like that? Your mother?"

"She didn't teach us to make the bed."

"Why not?"

"She was busy. There. In you go now."

"That's right," she said, her eyes closed. "I forgot you were masterful."

The radio was playing some slow Nelson Eddy thing.

"Come on," I said. I came over and took her hands, and she let me pull her to her feet.

"I'm so tired," she said, and leaned against me. She put her arms around my neck and hung from it like a necklace, rocking a little. We started rocking from foot to foot together to the music.

"You got yourself all snug in here," she said. "A real little nest."

"I like having a nice place to stay."

"Sure. You were on the tramp once. I forgot."

"That's okay."

"Weren't you afraid? Out there?"

"Of what?"

"I dunno. Getting hurt."

"A little. Not much. Hurt never lasts. What doesn't last doesn't mean anything."

"Then I guess you think nothing means anything much, because I don't know anything that lasts. I don't even think death'll last. I think when it comes, it'll be as crappy and slipshod as everything else."

"Yeah?"

"I think it'll fall apart in an afternoon like a pair of cheap stockings."

"Then what?"

"I don't know. What are you trying to do, foxtrot?"

"I wouldn't know how."

"Why are you even listening to me?"

"Who says I'm listening?"

It was a new song now, and we weren't even trying to keep time anymore, just shuffling in circles.

"Yeah," I said, "I was afraid. When I was on the road. That's why I joined up. I was afraid if I kept rattling around like that, I'd die."

"Were you that starving?"

"I ate fine," I said impatiently. "Sometimes I went a day or two without, but that doesn't kill you. I don't mean starve, I mean just die. Just go rattling around from town to town for years and years until you're too sorry to waste a bullet on. Just go on forever. That's what I mean by dying. I don't ever want to do that again."

"All right. Don't get excited."

"All right," I said.

"You're not dead yet. We're not dead yet."

"No."

"Let's go to bed," she said.

"All right."

We kept circling around.

"It was little different this morning," I said.

"Uh huh."

"You were trying to get a little . . . "

"I guess," she said.

"Sorry."

"I listen to the same songs on the radio as everyone else," she said. "Sometimes I still want those things, too. You've got a lot. I thought maybe you might have something for me."

"I wish I did."

"I wish somebody did," she said.

It was hard to hear that 'somebody.'

"All right," I said. "Then I hope somebody does, too."

She kissed me. She wasn't kissing me because she thought I might like a kiss, or because she thought it'd be a good idea to kiss me just then, or because she knew a lot about kissing and she'd figured out just how I wanted it, or anything like that. She just kissed me. It went on for quite a while, and then she laid her head against my chest.

"Uh huh," she said.

"I guess," I said.

"Ray?"

"Yeah?"

"You think you'll ever marry?"

"I don't know."

"You wouldn't marry me? If you could?"

I shook my head. She felt my chin going back and forth against her hair.

"No?" she said.

"You've got the best little jungle-gym in the world, honey. But I'd get bored climbing around on it all by myself."

"And yesterday you thought you loved me."

"What if I do? Love doesn't help boredom."

"What does it help?" she said. "You'd think it'd help something."

I kissed the tip of her nose. It was delicate and finely made. I thought again how, if someone had really punched her there last night, it would've been swollen twice the size now, and too painful to touch. I supposed she'd poked a stick or something up there to make it bleed. And Shade's shirt had been powder-scorched. I couldn't see him letting Halliday in close enough for that. But getting in close would be no problem for Rebecca. I could see her taking Shade by the hand, leading him round back of the pump house, looking up at him soft-eyed, the way she was looking at me now. Her gun, when I'd checked it last night, had been freshly cleaned. That morning, it'd been full of crud. I guessed there wasn't much doubt that she'd killed Shade herself. There probably wasn't too much doubt as to why, either.

"Becky?" I said. "You sure you want to go through with this?"

She said, "I've never been so sure."

I kissed her hair and closed my eyes. We kept dancing.

24

Hanged Man

Rebecca said she was hungry again that evening and, like I said, I made us a big spaghetti dinner, but she didn't do much to it. She chewed her lip as much as she chewed anything else. She was getting nervy. I wasn't too pleased with things myself. I had fourteen hours left, about, and no traveling money to speak of. I did the washing up and then sat her down beside me and said, "Look. If we're going to do this, we'd better do it."

"Oh, now he's in a hurry," she said airily. "I guess he's tired of this."

She was coming unraveled, all right.

"Are you sure this is what you want?"

"Don't keep asking me that."

"If it's what you want, sooner is better."

"You're tired of me. You're all tired out. You're a tired old man," she said, climbing into my lap and making herself small.

"When's the next time the safe will be full?" I said, and kissed her shoulder.

"I could find out," she said.

"Could you find out tonight?"

She thought. "Yes. Sure. I know who to see. I'll go see

them tonight. I guess you want to get me out of here and get some sleep."

"I'm going to find a car we can use."

"You've got a car," she said.

"I'm not going to use my own car, Rebecca."

"Where are you going to get a car?"

"There are a lot of cars in Los Angeles."

"You know how to do that?"

"It's not hard."

"What if somebody notices it in the lot?"

"Rebecca, it's not going to be in the lot. Let me earn my money, all right?"

Clothes were a problem. All she had left was that brassiere. It had a few speckles of blood on it, but it was a real work of engineering and I don't know what you'd have had to do to really hurt it. I offered to drive over to her room and fetch her some clothes, but she said no. She put on the brassiere and posed.

"There," she said. "Now I think I'm all ready to go out. I think I look very nice now. Very stylish. How do I look?"

"Overdressed."

I picked my old shirt off the floor and buttoned her into it as she beamed up to me.

"Now," she said. "Now I know I'm ready to go out. What, you don't like it? You want to put more clothes on me? Mister Corson, I wonder if you really like girls."

"Why don't I go get some of your clothes?"

"No. No, I'd rather you didn't go back there."

I got out a pair of my dungarees. She was pretty much all legs, so the length wasn't a problem once we'd cuffed them, but each pants leg was big enough for all of her. I had a coil of rope in my closet next to my tools, and I cut a length and slipped it through the belt loops and pretty much tied her into my clothes. There was nothing to do about shoes. I gave her a few pairs of heavy socks and she put them on. "How're your feet?" I asked.

"They're fine," she said.

They were pretty torn up, but she'd forgotten about them. Her body was just something she hauled around like a suitcase. She went over to the mirror on my dresser and twisted around, trying to get a good look at herself.

"This is wonderful," she said. "I'm like a scarecrow. It's like Halloween. Look, you can't see anything," she said, and gave herself a little shake.

"Pretty good," I said.

"This is wonderful. I'm going to dress like this all the time from now on."

"Think so?"

"I'm sure of it. I've decided."

"I'm going to miss you," I told her.

"Well. I wish you hadn't said that. I don't know what to say to that."

"I didn't say it for you to say anything back to," I said, getting a little hot.

"I'm sorry, Ray." She lay her palm on my cheek. "You were good to me. You've been good to me."

So I figured I had those two things now: that kiss from before, and her hand on my cheek. And maybe the dance. Three things.

She kissed me again when the taxi came, like I was her best beau but she had other things to think about, and gave me a little toodle-oo wave from the back window as the cab pulled out. I went back in, packed a suitcase, and put it in the trunk of my car, along with my tools. I took my gun from the desk and put it in my holster. I looked around the room. The dishes were still stacked up in the drainer by the sink. I put them away in the cabinet and left. This time I didn't bother locking the door.

The place I wanted was on Sunset. I remembered it as just a couple blocks west of Western, but they're never where you remember them and I spent a while cruising back and forth before I clicked. The sign just said SUPPLIES & NOVELTIES. The show window was a little on the empty side. In front of a purple velvet curtain someone had set out a row of different-shaped candles in holders, a row of goblets set with glass jewels, and a figurine of a kneeling woman with a cat's head.

Inside the place was a lot cheerier. The woman at the cash register was a little witchy-looking, which might have been what gave her the idea to get into the business. She was in her thirties somewhere, dressed in beat chick clothes, a black turtleneck and a peasant skirt, and she smiled when I came in. The place smelled pretty strong of incense.

"Quite a place here," I said.

"Thanks," she said.

"Pretty good business?"

"I'm not in it for the fresh air and sunshine," she said contentedly. "I do okay."

"Your place?"

"That's right."

"You keep it nice," I said truthfully. It was all spic and span. She had rows of Mason jars full of powders and dried leaves, all neatly labeled: Shave Grass, Hyssop, Hemlock Bark, Borage, Hibiscus. There was a box full of horseshoes. There was a glass case full of incense burners stamped out of brass and tin, and everything with pentagrams on it, even what looked like table napkins, and Ouija boards and Junior Ouija Boards with big colored letters. I said, "I guess people want answers, huh?"

"Guess they do."

"You do this kind of thing yourself? Foretell the future?" I set my hand down in front of her, palm up, and looked hopeful.

She slapped lightly at my arm. "Now, you'd better be

nice," she said. "That kind of stuff is just out of books, anyway. It's not what's in the lines, it's what's in the person who reads them. What she sees."

"What she sees? Just by looking?"

"Sure. If you're good."

"You can just look at someone and see how he'll wind up?"

"Well, it's more you see a sort of light around someone. And in that light, certain pictures come to you, or ideas. And sometimes they're what's going to happen."

She'd been gazing like I was something far off she was trying to get into focus.

"What do you see right now?" I said.

She looked away. "I don't mean I can see things, personally. I mean, maybe you've got a talent, or think you do, but you still have to develop it," she said uncomfortably.

"No time, huh? Business keeps you hopping?"

"That's right."

"You have any books on the Tarot?"

"Sure. Back over there by the antlers. Third shelf."

She was watching me again. She didn't seem as jaunty somehow.

I went where she said and took down a book called *The Silver Horn Guide to the Tarot*. It was by one "Third Dreamer," complete with double quotes around the name. On the jacket there was something that looked sort of like a diagram of a molecule labeled with numbers and Hebrew letters, and beneath a line in tiny type: *And I saw a strong Angel proclaiming with a loud voice, Who is worthy to open the Books and loose the seals thereof?* I opened it and flipped the pages until I found a picture of the upside-down guy in the tree.

I read:

MAJOR ARCANA
{KEY 12}
THE HANGED MAN

A Man is hanged by his foot from a Tau-cross of Living Wood. His arms form a Triangle pointing Downward; his legs a Cross. He nears but has not attained the Freedom of the World {Key 21}; his task is Surrender to Death and Resurrection. Through the Cycle from 1 to 10 God guides His Child's Hands, now the chisel is placed in the hands of the Matured Youth who must shape the Man To Be. Correspondences: the Moon {Key 18}, the Brow Chakra, the High Self, the 12 Signs of the Zodiac, the 12 Labors of Hercules. Viz. the mediæval custom of BAFFLING *by which Debtors were hanged by the Foot sometimes prior to Execution.*

§ The suspended Mind, governed by the Law of Reversal. Material Temptation. Paradox, difficulty. Remote Intervention. A Sacrifice may be required for Redemption. Punishment, Loss. Fatal and not voluntary. Suffering generally.

Reversed: Arrogance. Willfulness. Resistance to Wisdom, sunken in physical Matters. Wasted Effort. False Prophecy.

Let not the waters on which thou journeyest wet thee. —A. CROWLEY

I closed the book and stood there rubbing my nose. The gal at the cash register hadn't stopped watching me. By now her eyes were about as sad as eyes got. "Do you want that book," she said, almost whispering.

I shook my head and put it back on the shelf.

"Can I do anything for you."

"No," I said.

She whispered, "Then I think I'd like you out of my store now, please."

25

Rebecca

Halliday's house still didn't look like much house for a gangster. But one good thing about it, no one seemed to be home. No lights, no cars in the driveway. I'm not sure what I'd have done if someone had been there. I turned left at the corner and left again onto Remsen Avenue, which ran parallel to Shippie and one block over, and decided on a house that was being renovated, not quite back to back with Halliday's but only three doors down, with a few trees in between. I pulled into the driveway, and got my toolkit from the trunk, making no special attempt to be quiet. I went into the new garage, which had no door yet. It was just half-naked studs letting in the moonlight. I set down my tools and put on some gloves. I wiped down my flashlight and gun, in case I had to leave them inside. I put the flashlight in my pocket and my gun in my holster, then slipped out through the open studs at the back of the garage and made my way through the trees to Halliday's back door.

I was prepared to go back and get my bolt-cutters, but he hadn't put the chain on and my little strips of Samoan lagoon were all I needed. I stopped inside the door and held my breath. The house was still. If there was anyone there, they were asleep and not snoring. Or else holding their breaths and waiting for me with guns. I stood there with my eyes closed, letting Rebecca's map come back to me. When I had it clear in my mind and my eyes were used to blackness, I opened them. It's good to have a flashlight, but it's better not to use it, and I walked through the dark kitchen into what I knew was the dining room.

Rebecca's map seemed to be pretty damn good. I peeked through a side door and flashed my light in, just to check, and there were rows of 16mm projectors in carrying cases, just as she'd said. I closed the door softly and went through an archway into the front parlor. In the middle was a big armchair with antimacassars. I flicked the flash on it. It was upholstered in roses and green leaves. I looked through the side door there, not using the light. I saw a small room with a single bed and a movie camera in the corner on a stand.

I got out my gun and went slowly upstairs, stepping on the edges of the risers beside the wall. I still made little noises. You always do. Near the top of the stairs I peered through the banister and found all the doors open. The rooms seemed empty. I strode up the rest of the stairs, not caring about what noise I made, and stalked from room to room, gun first. Nobody. I decided I was probably okay and began going over the rooms in earnest.

The one near the head of the stairs was a bathroom, and there was nothing in it out of the ordinary. Next to it was a small room someone had fitted out with metal shelves. There were cans of film on the shelves, each can neatly labeled. I closed the curtain on the window and put on the flash. *Surprise for Auntie*, with Big Betsy, Rita, and Ramón. *Just A Beginner*, with Sandra and Ramón. *Penny's Punishment*, with Marilyn and The Sheik. *Betsy Gets It Good*, with Ramón, The Sheik, and Big Betsy. There was a row of big looseleaf books that seemed to record which copies of which film had been checked out to whom. I closed them and went into the next room.

This was a back bedroom with a frilly cream-colored bedspread. The walls were painted peacock blue and almost bare. The night table held an inlaid jewelry box, but there was nothing in it but a few pieces of costume stuff. I opened the closet and found low-cut evening dresses on hangers. I took down a couple of hatboxes and found hats. I opened the lingerie drawer and found lingerie. I went into the next room, which seemed to be the master bedroom. The curtains were closed, and I turned on my flash again.

In the middle of the room was a queen-sized bed. At the foot was a projector on a stand. The bed's headboard had been removed, and a white rectangle painted on the wall behind it. I went over to the projector and switched it on. There was that grinding ticking noise, and then a short length of number leader, and then the following appeared on the wall over the bed:

Prestige Enterprises Presents
THREE ON A MATCH

The next frame read:

Starring
BIG BETSY
ESMERALDA
THE SHEIK

Then:

ANOTHER DULL SUMMER AFTER NOON
BIG BETSY IS BORED WHAT TO DO?

Then Rebecca was sitting in the big flowered armchair in the living room I'd just left, with light pouring through the windows. It made her eyelids look translucent. She wore a dressing gown and high heels. Aside from that, she seemed to be waiting for a train. Someone behind the camera must have told her to smile, so she smiled at the camera, then stopped. Then she got up and slipped out of the gown. She lifted her breasts with her hands and then stood there bouncing them in her palms as if wondering what they'd fetch by the pound.

The door to the side room opened and a small dark woman entered, wearing only buckled shoes and those little ooh-la-la black ankle-stockings, and beaming like a prom queen on a parade float. Rebecca stooped to kiss her and Esmeralda began massaging her vigorously with both hands. I watched for a minute more, then switched off my flash, put it in my pocket, and stuck my gun in its holster. I began searching the room in the flickering light from the projector.

In the night table I found a small flat case with some silver cufflinks. I put it in my pocket. I found a cigarette lighter that was probably just nickel, but I'd lost mine and I took it and closed the drawer. There didn't seem to be anything in the dresser but clothes. The closet was a big one. I'd search it last. There was a small picture on the wall of a sailboat slipping past a lighthouse, heading out to sea. I looked behind it, looked at the back of it. I checked all the pictures and found a key taped to the back of one of them. I put it in my pocket. I got down on my hands and knees to look under the bed.

When I stood up, I saw that Esmeralda was gone and The Sheik was on the job. He was a bit of a runt, and wore an actual black mask across his eyes. It looked like he'd cut two holes in a black necktie. He was doing what he could to earn his pay, giving it his all, the cords in his neck jerking, and I saw that beneath him, Rebecca's face had smoothed out, the way a cat's face smoothes out when you stroke back the fur on its head, and that her body was rippling like a flag in a high wind. I wondered sadly what he had that I didn't. Just then I smelled that scent of plain harsh soap, the kind you'd do the laundry with, and slowly turned around. Rebecca stood just behind me in a simple pale evening gown, cut steeply down the front. Her mouth was slightly loose, and you could see the gleam of her teeth. Her face was still. Her little chrome .32 was staring at me, but she was staring at her own image on the screen. Her nipples stood out like a pair of steel pegs. Well, I thought, there's your answer.

Halliday stepped out of the shadows behind her.

"Put your hands in your back pockets," he said. "All the way, palms in. That's good." He sidled over without hurry and slipped the gun out of my holster. He did it right, and there wasn't a moment when he was blocking Rebecca's shot. Then he walked around the bed and flopped into an armchair with the gun in his lap. He rubbed his eyes and didn't say anything more.

"Huh," I said. "I thought I'd hear if somebody came in."

"The room's soundproof," he said. "You should've left the door open."

"I thought I did."

"It swings shut."

"Live and learn," I said.

"Learn, anyway," he said. "Any luck finding the safe full of gold?"

"Ah, I wouldn't know how to open a safe, anyway. I was hoping for something more like the silverware. I needed traveling money and I figured you two owed me something."

"It's just stainless. How come you didn't come kill me with Becky like you were supposed to?"

"I got tired of your sister's stories, Jimmy."

We listened to the projector whir.

"Your sister Rebecca," I said. "She tells too many stories."

Rebecca stirred and took her eyes off the movie. She gazed at me like I was the sky and somebody told her there was a ring around the moon.

I said, "I've got a few cop connections, and they got me James Lee Marron. And the thing about Marron, he's got a kid sister. One Rebecca Anne Marron, a local beauty queen and, ah." I looked at her. "Championship swimmer. You can see the resemblance if you look. You've both got the same color hair. I'm gonna scratch my nose now."

I took my hand from my pocket, slowly, scratched my nose, and gave my face a good rub. Then I put my hand back in my pocket.

"Here's how I see it," I said. "You're sick of smut. You're sick of the small time. This place is mortgaged to the doorknobs. You've been hoping to move a little powder—just hoping, so far—but around here, that's all Scarpa's. Maybe if you killed him, you could get a piece, but why would Burri let you? Well, let's think. Everyone knows Scarpa hates your guts. What if he had some goon try to chill you? Only you got lucky and chilled the goon instead, and then ran to Burri and said, Grampa, look, a dead goon, don't we get to hit Scarpa back? You've been putting together a little army—the one you tried recruiting me for, the one I saw meeting here Wednesday night. You were just about ready. All you needed was Burri's okay. And your sister wanted her big brother to have his day in the sun. So she left her nice little peacock-blue room here, checked into a boarding house, and started looking around for someone to play Scarpa's goon. Somebody who wouldn't be missed."

"I'd put my baby sister in the middle like that?"

"Halliday, you useless son of a bitch," I said. "You never put anything anywhere. The only idea you ever had is ask a girl to take her drawers down. Rebecca's the one with the ideas. This was her play. Shade was her first pick for my spot, but she found he wouldn't kill, even for her. So she scratched around until she got me, and then I even signed on with Scarpa, which made the setup nice and tight. But somehow I didn't seem too eager, either. So now she's got two of us. She had to get rid of one and move the other off the dime. So she took Shade for a drive, put four beans under his breast pocket with her shiny little gun, ripped up her dress, and came pounding on my door, crying, You wouldn't kill the bad man, and now look. But Jesus, Becky, remember? I'm the boy who's always going through your purse."

"If you checked my gun," she said dully, "you saw it hadn't been fired."

I shook my head. "Next time, don't just clean the barrel. Next time, break the gun and clean the block. And don't leave a lace hanky stained with gun oil not twenty feet from the body."

Halliday sighed. "I said you were getting too fancy, Beck."

"Fancy, hell. Incompetent. Like driving up in a new blue Stude and explaining to me how you were broke. Maybe you thought I was nearsighted. Maybe you just didn't know where to get a cheap car."

"There is no right side of the tracks in Porter," Rebecca said slowly. "I know where to get cheap things. I knew where to get you."

"Sure," I said. "I'm cheap. But I'm not sloppy. All this vaudeville, and how were you thinking of selling it to Burri? If Scarpa wanted to kill you, Halliday, he'd get Burri's blessing in advance. Burri's not giving you Scarpa's territory. Burri thinks you're an animal. He wouldn't give you your own watch as a graduation present. Jesus, I feel sorry for you two. You've both flopped at everything you ever tried since high school, and now you're flopping at this. And you know it. And all you could think of to do, honey, is take me to bed and hope I'd quit asking questions. I practically had to push you out the door tonight, but I figured if I gave you half an excuse, you'd go see your brother."

"Why's that?" Halliday said.

"You were lonely for each other. You hadn't seen each other in days." I shrugged. "You were lonely for each other."

It was quiet again, except for the ticking of the projector. Halliday was massaging the bridge of his nose with his thumb and forefinger. All the hoods watch gangster movies, and that's where most of them get the bored and weary bit, but he really did look beat. I guess we were all pretty tired. "We're the second and third of six," he said dreamily. "And you know? The others turned out straight as a goddamn die."

He looked over at Rebecca. She was watching the movie.

"Jesus Christ," he said, "will you turn that crap off?"

I stooped obediently and reached for the power cord. Halliday said, "Not you," and Rebecca screamed, "You'll break it," and I yanked on the cord, sending the projector teetering on its stand.

They still weren't that far from Porter, and one of those Bell & Howells costs money. For a moment, it's all they were looking at.

Then I was behind Rebecca, hugging her hard around the ribs, her gun hand in mine.

She woke up when the projector hit the floor. She was a hundred and twenty pounds of wildcat then. But she was only a hundred and twenty pounds of wildcat, and I had a good grip on her by the time Halliday came round the bed. I knew he wouldn't risk a shot. A .44 goes right on through. He held my gun by the barrel, ready to club. The projector was grinding against the rug, lighting our legs and the dust ruffle of the bed. Our faces were shadows. When Halliday got next to us, I spun Rebecca around, brought her gun hand up, and pressed her finger down on the trigger.

The muzzle was against his ribs. The shot was no louder than a book slamming shut.

Halliday looked at me, as if he wanted to ask what I'd just done, but didn't know quite how to put it. Then he looked at Rebecca and his lips moved, and his eyes seemed to want to reassure her.

Then his knees went, and his face dipped forward onto her breast.

He slid down her body to the floor.

I spun Rebecca around again and shot out the window. "Help!" I screeched, "Police! Help! Help!" It wasn't very good, but it didn't have to be. I fired into the ceiling, floor, walls, and bed until the hammer clicked. Then I let her go.

Rebecca stared straight ahead, still holding the gun, a black streak of blood down her belly. Gradually, she lowered her shadowed face and looked down at her brother. She looked at him for maybe a minute. Then she looked back up at the wall again and gazed at that little sailboat sailing past the lighthouse.

I elbowed the bedside lamp onto the floor. Rebecca didn't seem to hear it smash. I sat down on the bed and twisted around on my rear, to get the covers mussed, and then I got up and took hold of Rebecca's shoulders and shook her. She dropped the gun. I took hold of a shoulder strap and ripped it down. She blinked and stopped looking at the little sailboat. Palms isn't Beverly Hills, but if you call the police, they come, and I heard sirens now, very faint in the distance.

Her hair still didn't look right, so I ruffled it with my fingers. She was looking at me now.

"You," she said. "You've."

She licked her lips and blinked.

"I don't," she said.

She reached out slowly with both hands, as if she wasn't sure where I was, and found my chest. She sort of petted it.

"We," she said.

She ran out of breath and licked her lips. "We could . . ."

I once saw a cat half-squashed on the side of the road, the front half still trying to crawl. I turned from her and went over to the projector, which was grinding away on the floor and smelling hot. I nudged the cord with my foot until the light went out. I didn't want a fire. The room seemed very quiet now. The sirens were faint, but getting louder. "I know," I said, not looking at her. "I know you weren't just acting the other night. The night that Shade, the night you killed him. I kept telling you. Murder isn't a lark. I guess you know now. I know, I know it was difficult."

I had no idea what I was talking about, and I stopped.

I turned and, without looking at her, went over and knelt by Halliday's body. I started taking off his rings.

"You were robbed," I said, keeping my eyes on what I was doing. "You're very beautiful. And you're, you're a good actress. You could've made me think you loved me, could've done it easily. But you didn't. Thank you for that, anyway."

I stopped again. I was sweating pretty badly.

She hunkered down and began petting my back, clumsily, with both hands.

I got up and she flinched away from me. Her eyes were wide and senseless. I took her by the shoulders and led her over to where she'd been standing. The sirens were getting louder. I pulled off my right glove and started to put on Halliday's rings.

"All right," I said. My mouth didn't want to work properly. I was trying to keep in mind which order he wore his rings in. "I think that about does it," I said. "The police'll be able to tell someone else was here, if they look hard enough. I don't think they'll look too hard. Between Halliday's record, the movies, the match between the bullets in Shade's body and his, the mark of his rings on your face . . . "

" . . . my face . . . " she said.

"Maybe you can sell them on the idea of looking," I said. "It's possible. You're a good little saleswoman."

She licked her lips and set her hands on my chest.

"You've got a fighting chance," I told her. "That's more than you gave Lorin Shade. It's more than you were going to give me. Goodbye, Rebecca."

By then I'd worked the last of his rings onto my right hand. I made a fist and drove it into her jaw.

I'd meant to just let her drop, but I couldn't stop myself from catching her halfway and easing her down. I looked at her lying there and decided I hadn't spoiled it. The way the gun had fallen looked about right. I bent over Halliday again and put the rings back on his fingers, giving each one a wipe as I did. I tugged his lapels around a bit and cuffed his dead face hard, frontways and backhand. The sirens were pretty loud now. I picked up my own gun and flashlight and had a last look around. It all seemed okay. Halliday was right: it's best not to get too fancy. I slipped out the back door, locking it behind me,

and was in my car, pulling out onto Remsen, by the time
the police turned onto Shippie. It all went about as well
as you could have hoped for.

26
The Special

The guy with the load of avocados was nice to me and
went a few miles out of his way to let me off at a diner he
knew outside Gault, Nevada, where it was cheap, he said,
and they treated you all right. I thanked him and got
down, and he started up again with a roar like you'd
pressed all the keys on a church organ at once. He made
a big U-turn that took him way off the shoulder on either
side and headed back the way he came. Then there was
nothing but the smell of diesel exhaust. It was a smell I
knew. The diner wasn't the kind gotten up to look like a
railroad car. It wasn't gotten up to look like anything, and
I couldn't help noticing the shape the roof was in. I was
tired enough that everything I looked at seemed to be
grainy and crawling. It was just past dawn, and the desert
was cold. The cold felt clean. I picked up my toolbox and
suitcase. My typewriter was still on my desk at the
Harmon Court. Round Head could give it to his kids to
play with. The door jingled as I pushed through, awk-
wardly because of my bag and toolkit, and the waitress
looked up. It was just me and her in the place.

We said good morning and I asked if there was somewhere I could wash my face.

When I got back she came over and I ordered the
thirty-cent breakfast special. There wasn't even a cook.
Once she had my order, she went behind the counter to

fix it herself. She moved without hurrying. Twenty years ago she'd been the prettiest girl in Gault or some other little town. Now she had a little extra around the hips and still no ring that I could see. The ceiling sagged pretty badly by the steam table, and looked like it had for a while. I wondered where I was going to sleep.

She came back and set my order down: three eggs up, home fries, four link sausages, and rye toast, all on thick, chipped plates, plus a big glass of orange juice and a coffee in a cup with a blue stripe around it. She gave me the rag end of a smile as I tucked in.

It was all good, and the coffee was better. When I finished it I ordered the same all over again.

"You can eat," she said.

"When they let me," I said.

I put down the second breakfast and wiped my plate with bread, and she refilled my cup.

Then she stood beside me holding the pot. I was looking into my wallet. "Can you make it?" she said gently.

It seemed a long time since I'd heard anyone speak gently.

"Just about," I said.

She set the pot on the heater and came back over. She sat herself down across from me. You could tell it felt good for her to get off her feet. I put down my wallet.

"Looks like you work with your hands," she said.

I looked down at them myself. That when I noticed it, a dark gold hair on the sleeve of my jacket.

She watched me pick it off and drop it on the floor.

"What do you need done?" I said.

THE
END